PUNISHMENT FOR POPPY

by

ARABELLA ORTIZ

Published by **CHIMERA**
ISBN 9781780807584

Chapter 1

The day that was to throw eighteen-year-old Poppy Cavendish's life into tumultuous change started like every other she could remember, with the tolling of the Maidenhall College bell in its little clock tower above the headmistress's quarters at six-thirty a.m. sharp. The girl rose effortlessly from sleep, opened wide green eyes, and sat up so abruptly that her breasts gave a softly firm bounce. Barely conscious of this, she stared glumly at the empty dormitory with its twin rows of neatly made-up beds and thought about the prospect of yet another lonely day with nothing very much to do.

Poppy realised she had dreamt about Karen Stringfellow again, her absent American friend who was on her summer holidays back in the States and who, during term, slept in the bed next to hers. Too ashamed and surprised to want to recall the details of the dream, she was glad of the diversion when she heard a creak on the stairs outside the dormitory, even though she knew it preceded the arrival of Miss Brady, the strict housemistress and one of the few staff who stayed at the college during the summer holidays.

'Time to get out of that bed, Cavendish.' Miss Brady marched into the dormitory clapping her hands in a forceful, domineering manner. Usually a cold, distant figure, she stood so close to Poppy's bed that the nearness of the strong limbs beneath her skirt made the girl feel somewhat uncomfortable. 'It's one of Captain Smythe's regular inspection days today, so you'll be unsupervised for most of it,' she said. 'So I'm trusting you to keep out of the way and behave yourself.'

This tediously regular event had Poppy wondering why Captain Smythe was at the college so often as Miss Brady's severe form swept out of the room, but as the girl shook her long, russet hair she thought, big deal, for she was due to be leaving the college for good at any time in the very near future - hopefully in the next few weeks - and then such trivialities as college inspections would not bother her again. This made her think of her imminent departure into the world outside the brick-walled boundaries of Maidenhall College, and although it was July it was a cool morning and she shivered as she got up and padded through to the adjoining to washroom. For once Poppy was glad of the strict dress code at Maidenhall, for the shapeless cotton nightdresses that the headmistress, Miss Sharpe, chose personally for her girls were nothing if they were not warm.

Oblivious to the fact that no matter how shapeless her nightie was it could not quite disguise the voluptuous curves of her body, Poppy pulled it over her head and stepped gingerly into the shower. The water was scarcely tepid and she squealed as it took her breath away for a moment, and her creamy skin soon displayed a covering of goose bumps. Her nipples stiffened as though imbued with a will of their own, and though she washed quickly because of the cold she was conscious of a disquieting tingle as she soaped between her legs. Unaware of the erotic spectacle she presented as she turned off the flow of water and wrapped a towel around herself, beneath her armpits for the sake of warmth, she hurried to the line of washbasins and bent over one to brush her teeth.

Miss Sharpe, the college headmistress, was vigilant in discouraging the sin of vanity in the girls in her charge, and full-length mirrors were banned at the college. Like all the Maidenhall girls, Poppy was made to dress and undress under cover of her nightgown, so that her body was relatively undiscovered territory even to her. But unwrapping the towel and standing naked without the steely eye of a lecturer upon her, she caught sight of her breasts in one of the face mirrors fixed to the washroom wall. After a quick look around to make sure she was unobserved, she stood on tiptoe and inquisitively cupped the perfect globes in her palms for a better look. Each was tipped with a pink rivet of flesh that she turned curiously between her fingers and thumbs.

'Oh!'

Poppy felt an echo of the sensation she had experienced whilst washing her intimate parts in the shower, and clenched her thighs hard together. Instead of giving her relief, though, this made the mysterious tingle return even more insistently.

Feeling exposed and chilly, but also excited by her nakedness, she scampered into the dormitory where she rubbed herself dry and warmed herself up, with another, dry institutional towel that felt as rough as sandpaper.

When dry she took her uniform from her locker, fully intending to put it on, but in the months leading up to that fateful day, Poppy, feeling the restless tingle that pulsed between her legs, had often wished for privacy so she could investigate its source. Now, she realised, she had the perfect opportunity to do just that. If Miss Brady returned before breakfast the creaking stair would give her away, and by the time she came through the door into the dormitory Poppy would hope to be primly pulling on her knickers. With her decision made to give in to temptation there came a dark, forbidden thrill, and throwing caution to the wind she slipped back into bed, still naked.

She ran her hands over her breasts, shivered with delight at the sensation this caused, then turned her nipples between fingers and thumbs and ground her thighs together, making pleasurable sensations permeate her body as the intimate area between her legs was deliciously stimulated.

Lifting the bedclothes with both hands, Poppy stared down at her pubic mound. Nestled within its soft wisps of hair she could see her tender outcrop of flesh, the source of the pleasure that radiated through her body. Wetting two fingers in her mouth, she gripped this little promontory of pink flesh and tentatively thrummed it.

'Oh... oh... *oh!*'

Poppy's gasps of pleasure were muted, but drifted around the dormitory walls and windows in a way that added to her excitement. Magically, the flesh that was the focus of her attention and joy was growing wetter and wetter. She stopped stimulating it to explore the little valley at whose head it lay, and searched for the source of the slippery juice that covered the petals of flesh as dew coats a morning flower. She probed inquisitively, and then returned her attentions to the juicy folds at which she had mischievously begun, spreading the tender lips and exploring the inner depths with a curious fingertip.

Again she located the tiny protuberance there. It was as hard as a midwinter bud, but so wickedly sensitive that she touched it only fleetingly. Instead she placed her hands flat on either side of the fleshy outcrop and moved them towards one another until it was trapped between her forefingers. Then she moved her hips sinuously up and down, and her hands around and around until she settled into a rhythm that made her pleasure grow inexorably. Then, finding herself in urgent need of mental stimulation to accompany this teasing activity, she allowed the previous night's dream about her best friend, Karen Stringfellow, to return to the forefront of her fantasies, and gave herself up to its naughty secrets.

In her dreams they had come in from playing hockey and flopped back perspiring on their beds, and though Poppy could not remember them pulling off their East House tops, she recalled their excitement as they rubbed naked breasts together, crushing nipple against nipple.

Gazing dreamily at her slender hand as it turned in her nest of pubic hair, she felt anew the ardour with which she had dreamt of sucking the tender tips of Karen's breasts. As Poppy's hand moved with growing delight her shapely hips instinctively writhed with greater intensity, as though fucking, though in reality the innocent girl had never done such a thing.

She began to fantasise that it was not her finger but Karen's that was frigging her, and jerked the bedclothes down with her feet until her breasts were exposed. The sight of their rhythmic quiver caused her excitement to mount even more until she felt that a climax of some kind was imminently near.

With growing excitement she imagined that her hand was working deep between her American friend's legs, that they were kissing, panting the breath of passion into each other's open mouth...

But as her orgasm encroached with overwhelming sweetness her bliss turned to horror as a dark shadow loomed and filled the dormitory doorway.

'So this is how you repay my trust, is it?' The formidable figure of Miss Brady marched into the room, clutching her bunch of keys tightly, as she had done to stop them jangling when she stepped over the annoyingly creaky step on the building's main wooden staircase.

'I-I wasn't doing anything, miss!' Poppy stuttered, desperately snatching the bedclothes back up over her naked breasts. 'I got back into bed because I was... um... because I was feeling a little... a little unwell, miss.'

'Oh yes, unwell are we?' Miss Brady's sneering expression was one of extreme scepticism. 'Well it's my belief that you've been touching yourself, *down there.* Between your legs.' She stomped over to Poppy's bed and stared down at her with piercing eyes. 'And if you have, the evidence will be plain to see.'

'E-evidence, miss?' Poppy stared up at the housemistress's imposing form with wide, frightened eyes.

'Yes, the evidence.' Without further warning the woman pushed Poppy flat on her back and ripped the bedclothes back out of her way. The helpless girl offered only a token resistance as the lecturer forced a hand between her legs, scooped a finger against her pussy and held it aloft, traitorously glistening with

4

incriminating juices. 'You're sopping wet!' she declared in triumph. 'Disgraceful! Get dressed, Cavendish, I'm taking you to see Miss Sharpe right away.'

'Miss Brady, *please...*' The girl's heartbeat quickened with renewed fear as she imagined being cast out of the college in disgrace, banished to the unknown world outside the tall stone walls without the guidance and support of the institution that had raised and educated her, and always looked after her welfare for as long as she could remember. 'I've never done anything like this before, miss, I promise I haven't.' She began to weep, swallowed hard and begged, 'C-can't you punish me yourself, now, here? Do we have to involve Miss Sharpe?'

'Hmm.' Miss Brady took Poppy's chin in her cupped hand and turned her tearstained face up to her own. As the girl's eyes stared pleadingly into hers she relented, and nodded slowly. 'Very well,' she said calculatingly. 'You could be right. Perhaps it would be better to nip this in the bud quickly. Fetch me one of your gym shoes.'

'Yes, miss, right away,' Poppy gasped. 'Thank you, miss.'

She slipped out of bed again and bent to pick up her nightdress, intending to cover her naked body for the walk to the lockers at the end of the dormitory.

'Put that down,' Miss Brady snapped. 'Since you're so fond of displaying your nakedness wantonly, you can remain as you are.'

Poppy blushed, feeling exposed and humiliated as she obeyed, but as she hurried the length of the dormitory and back she became conscious that she was experiencing a perversely naughty pleasure in her predicament. And worse was to follow when, to her shame, she felt a renewed tingle of sexual excitement pulsing between her legs as Miss Brady pulled a chair to the side of her bed, sat down with her legs open in a very masculine fashion, and held out an upturned hand for the gym shoe.

'Over my knee,' she ordered, and hesitating for only a moment, the girl obeyed meekly, lying across the black skirt with her long hair hanging down to the floor. The lecturer then immediately slapped the sensitive backs of Poppy's thighs, stinging blows that precipitated a fresh outburst of tears. 'Part your thighs, you shameless creature,' the housemistress ordered. 'I want to check that you're not getting some sort of despicable and perverse pleasure from this.'

'Yes... miss,' Poppy mumbled sorrowfully, and as she dutifully opened her legs she was horrified to feel yet another tiny thrill at the thought that the stern woman could see her most secret places. But her fleeting pleasure proved short-lived as Miss Brady raised the rubber-soled shoe, paused infinitesimally, and brought it down hard on each of her buttocks.

Slap... Slap!

The scalding double blow made Poppy squeal with pain, and the lecturer watched with evident satisfaction as livid imprints of the shoe's patterned sole rose angrily on the girl's creamy skin.

Then, as Poppy watched tears of confusion dripping to the floor, she was amazed to feel her tormentor parting her buttocks with feather-light fingertips, apparently to examine her anal region for some inexplicable reason.

'*Miss*,' Poppy whispered in alarm. 'Whatever do you think you're *doing?*'

'Don't you dare question my actions,' Miss Brady warned instantly. 'You will really suffer now for your impertinence.' She raised the rubber-soled shoe high in the air and brought it down again.

Slap, slap! Slap, slap!

Poppy's shapely bottom bucked desperately as a biting pain made her sob pitifully, and Miss Brady's eyes glinted with satisfaction as she watched four new blotchy imprints rise on the teenager's buttocks, their angry red in sharp contrast with the ivory flesh that surrounded them. One had landed above and one below the first livid patch on each buttock, and as they defined themselves into oval ridges of pain the lecturer coasted her palm over them, so gently that her hand barely touched, and Poppy had hardly got over her astonishment that Miss Brady could be so tender when the inquisitive hand slid into the region at the delta of her thighs.

'Oh, *miss*...' Too afraid to object again, she also lost her will to do so as her tormentor's middle finger gathered moisture from the elusive little entrance to her pussy's core, and spread it over her clitoris. As the teacher's finger moved around and around her erect bud with tantalising craft, the gorgeous teenager could only whisper, 'Oh, m-miss... that feels lovely, miss...'

'You wicked, wicked creature,' Miss Brady huskily admonished, when she saw that her charge's pleasure had gathered to the point where she was almost slipping into an orgasm, and then she raised the gym shoe again.

Slap! Slap! Slap! Slap! Slap!

The furious onslaught of blows made Poppy sob hopelessly and sag wearily over Miss Brady's stout thighs, and then the housemistress dropped the gym shoe and dragged the listless girl up to her feet.

Then standing herself, she grasped Poppy by the shoulders, turned her to face away from her and regarded her red, beaten buttocks with satisfaction.

'You haven't learnt one thing from this beating, have you?' she demanded, running her hands over the girl's scalded bottom, lecherously savouring its burning heat, and before Poppy's befuddled thoughts had a chance to compile a reply the robust woman put her arms around the girl's waist from behind, cupped her breasts and seized her nipples, revolving them slowly between her fingertips. And when the girl's hips began to slowly move instinctively back and forth in a natural response, the teacher snaked one hand downward, the middle finger extended, and sought out the erect bead that hid in folds of moist flesh between her beautiful student's legs.

'You're obviously in need of some serious one-to-one counselling,' she whispered urgently in the girl's ear. 'In need of some extra-curricula tutoring. You will come to my office after lunch, when we will start a very special course for you.'

'Y-yes... miss,' Poppy agreed timidly, knowing she had no alternative but to do so.

'Good... very good.' Satisfied with the response, the housemistress released her and started to walk towards the open door, but as Poppy watched her sheepishly, she stopped and turned back.

6

'I shouldn't be telling you this, Cavendish,' she said, catching Poppy's look and holding it steadily, 'but if you notice anything unusual as you go down for breakfast, do not on *any* account investigate further.' It seemed that a shadow passed over her authoritarian demeanour. 'There was a girl here once, not so very long ago, a foolish creature who chose to ignore my advice, and she's regretting it to this day, believe me.'

A moment later the woman had gone, and Poppy did not know what to make of her mysterious parting words as she pulled on her navy-blue knickers, their snug elastic biting into her waist and the tops of her creamy thighs, then as she clipped on her white bra and slipped into her crisply laundered white shirt, she heard the crunch of tyres on the gravel drive below, and doing up each shirt button in turn she looked down through the dormitory window just in time to see the distinguished chairman of the college governors step out of his Daimler.

'Captain Smythe,' Poppy whispered, as an unexpected and inexplicable instinct made her clench and relax her thighs and buttocks.

She watched his soldierly form stride up the three stone steps to the double front door and into the building, then stepped into her pleated navy-blue skirt, the hem only reaching down to just above mid-thigh.

The strange events of the morning had given Poppy serious food for thought, and because she had twice been taken almost to the point of sexual fulfilment, only to have it cruelly taken away from her on both occasions, the insistent tingle between her legs gave her no peace whatsoever.

She worried too about her imminent departure into the big wide world beyond the college boundaries, and because of such major physical and mental distractions she dawdled as she finished buttoning her shirt, distractedly toying with the top button, then bent from the waist with a natural easy grace to buckle the single strap on each of her black shoes.

The breakfast bell sounded as she tied a big knot in her tie, but still she did not hurry overly, because mealtimes were always lax during the holidays.

She had almost forgotten Miss Brady's strange warning by the time she skipped down the East House back stairs. During term time these were brightly lit, but in the holiday periods half the lights were switched off to conserve energy, and as she turned a ninety degree bend halfway down she noticed a tiny crack of light shining from the wainscot. Poppy stopped in her tracks. She then recalled the housemistress's mysterious words and knew she should investigate no further, but her curiosity was irresistibly strong - probably fuelled by the very warning that was supposed to quash any possible inquisitiveness.

It was clearly evident that the light was seeping through a tiny knothole in the oak panelling, and she argued defensively that no one would know even if she did take a little peek to satisfy her curiosity. Her heart began to beat furiously as she looked around to make sure she was unobserved, crept over to the source of light, got down on one knee and pressed her eye to the little aperture there.

Poppy was not surprised to find herself looking into the college gymnasium, which she had already assessed was on the other side of the wall, but she was amazed to find herself staring at three naked people grouped close by!

One of them was a slim dark girl. All three were visible only from the waist down, and the girl was at an angle and almost out of Poppy's range of vision, but she could see that she was tied facing the wall-bars, her body in a star shape and her round, olive-skinned bottom thrust back.

The other two were also standing with their backs to Poppy, facing the girl whom she now heard sobbing helplessly. One was a matronly woman with a large but shapely behind while the other, Poppy realised with a thrill that made her pussy tingle again, was a man!

His body told her he was at least middle-aged, and from his right hand a leather belt dangled. Poppy's breath caught in her chest when she saw this, and despite her shock she for some inexcusable reason longed to slip her hand into her tight blue panties and touch herself, but most of all she wanted him to turn around so she could see his front and his penis.

As she watched, fascinated, her mouth gaping, she heard him demand something in a voice as rough as gravel, and the girl reply defensively over her shoulder. Poppy could not make out their words, only the tone in which they were spoken, but it was obvious that the man was not satisfied by the girl's response.

He stepped forward, abruptly lashed her bare buttocks several times, and then stood back again. The woman then went to stand behind the bound and helpless girl, and snaked her hands around to her front with the obvious intention of fondling her breasts. At the same time she rubbed the front of her body in a sinuous, circular motion against the girl's punished behind. Then after a few breathless minutes of this lewd performance the pair changed places.

This time the woman held the belt and asked the questions, while the girl sobbed defensively as before. The only difference was that the woman put her hand to the front of the man's body as she spoke, and Poppy could see her arm moving back and forth, and it was obvious that she was caressing something there! Then she shouted accusingly and began flogging the girl's pert, outthrust bottom apparently without mercy. Her victim wailed, twisting her slim body desperately this way and that in a vain attempt to avoid the blows, and as Poppy watched she found that she could not help but slip her hand up her own skirt and rub her pussy through her knickers with her palm, when the woman eventually relented.

Now it was the man's turn to stand close behind the weeping girl, but instead of rubbing his body against her with a sort of circular motion as the woman had done before him, he thrust his hips forward and back, forward and back, over and over, his buttocks tensing and relaxing in unison with his movements. When he stopped he turned, holding his hand out for the belt, and Poppy had to quickly clamp her free hand over her mouth to smother the gasp that almost betrayed her forbidden presence at the spy hole as she caught her first glimpse of a rampant cock!

Utterly mesmerised and taken aback, her head in a total spin, she watched the man's erect organ nodding stiffly as he enthusiastically lashed the girl's shapely buttocks, and when his arm eventually stilled and lowered, and he turned and moved towards the peephole, she almost fled, fearful that she had been found out, but her legs suddenly seemed to be filled with lead and she could not move.

His cohort followed him, and before Poppy was able to gather her senses and take flight she caught a flash of a pair of large breasts with brown nipples descending as the woman turned her back on the man and bent to touch her toes. Her hair was dark, her head turned away, but although the watching girl could not see her face she had a clear view of her ample buttocks and the sexual folds that gaped just below them, covered with luxuriant black hairs.

The man advanced on her holding the base of his penis, and directed its bloated tip towards her pussy's centre, into which it sank with one lunge of his hips.

As Poppy rubbed more urgently against the dampening gusset of her blue knickers, she could hear the man and woman groaning and panting. She was surprised to see that even the slender girl tied to the wall-bars was gyrating her shapely bottom, apparently straining to look over her shoulder at the fornicating pair as she rubbed her sex against one of the horizontal bars.

The man reached around the woman and Poppy saw his finger appear between her legs, where it teased a hooded button of flesh that nestled there. Her own excitement had almost reached a crescendo when a door slamming upstairs made her straighten up sharply and hold her breath to listen for any worrying sounds of movement. Filled with trepidation as she remembered Miss Brady's warning, she decided it was time to get out of there, and hastily tiptoed down the remaining steps and out of East House into the bright college quadrangle.

Sunlight shone on ivy-covered walls and the sky was a faultless blue. Indeed, everything was so normal that the scene Poppy had just witnessed and her own shameful reaction to it seemed oddly out of place. Nevertheless, she could not help but wonder at what she had just seen and felt.

Although the regime at Maidenhall was harsh, as a sop to families of the girls the college kept a number of pet animals for the students to look after. There was no shortage of volunteers for this during term time, but in the holidays the few pupils who remained at the college had to take it in turns, and today it was Poppy's turn.

But as she fed the guinea pigs and cleaned out the rabbit hutches she was unable to shift the events of the morning from her mind, especially the stiff column of male flesh she had seen. After some minutes daydreaming about it she reminded herself that she was late for breakfast, and if she left it much longer it would all be cleared away and she'd have to go hungry until lunchtime, so she washed her hands quickly and scampered across the quad to the refectory.

The meal in the large oak-panelled room was a cheerless affair. Captain Smythe did not put in an appearance at the raised top table - which he usually did when visiting - where Miss Sharpe and Miss Brady sat eating and talking in hushed tones.

There was a smattering of other girls with nowhere to go for the holidays, but the only one of any interest to Poppy was Suky Desai, a pretty little creature with sparkling brown eyes who was also eighteen, though only just. Like Poppy she had no home or family, and at the end of the following term she would be waiting for Maidenhall College to find her a place in the world outside, just as Poppy was waiting now.

The two girls shared a chum in Karen Stringfellow, and could have relieved the boredom of holiday loneliness by getting better acquainted and spending time together, except for the college rule that forbade them from sitting together because Suky was a resident of West House while Poppy was a resident of East.

After breakfast Poppy went back up to the empty dormitory and sat looking out at the college grounds, unable to escape the anxiety she felt whenever she thought of her uncertain future, and then, feeling increasingly bored, she sneaked down to the pool for a forbidden, unsupervised swim, and having changed into her swimming costume and padded through to the pool she was surprised to see a sleek head bobbing up and down in the water, as dark as a seal's.

'Suky,' she called when she recognised the Eurasian girl's pretty face. 'How long have you been here?'

'Not long.' Suky waved her into the water, and the pair swam wordlessly for a time. Suky tired first and climbed effortlessly out of the pool, and Poppy did only a couple more lengths before she climbed out too and padded towards the changing booths, dripping water from her trim but shapely body as she went.

'Pssst!' Suky Desai's head appeared cheekily around a booth door, her liquid brown eyes large in the dimly lit changing room. 'Come in here, Poppy,' she said mischievously. 'We can share, if you like.'

The enormity of such a frowned-up act worried the usually obedient Poppy. 'But what if Old Sharpie turns up?' she whispered. 'Don't forget Captain Smythe is here today for one of his silly inspections, which means he'll almost certainly take a look in here at some point.' And then an even scarier prospect occurred to her, fuelled by her earlier perverse experience. 'Or Miss Brady, come to that.'

'Who cares?' Suky countered rebelliously. 'It's their own fault for leaving us unsupervised and with nothing to do.' So saying, she moved aside invitingly and coaxed Poppy closer. 'Come on, come in and share my cubicle!'

Suky was rubbing her slight body languidly with one of the rough college towels, and Poppy glanced at her shyly as she did slip inside the confined space. Her breasts were small but attractively plump with nipples the colour of raisins, making Poppy more aware of her larger, pale, pink-tipped orbs as she bashfully bent to dry her thighs.

'Oh...' Suky gasped as she eyed Poppy's breasts, neatly held within her wet swimming costume, 'you're so lucky, Poppy!'

'Lucky?' Poppy responded. 'Lucky about what?'

'Lucky to have such gorgeous boobs, of course,' Suky told her.

'But I always think they're too large,' Poppy objected.

'No, no, that's what men love.' Suky showed off her knowledge proudly. 'I sneaked a look at one of those girlie magazines at the newsagents in Maidenhall village not so long ago, and all the models had big boobs, so men must love them, or they wouldn't buy the magazines, would they?'

'No, I suppose not.' Poppy looked at herself with new eyes, for some reason wanting to tweak her nipples as she had done that morning but too shy to do so with Suky there. Then despite her reservations and despite feeling extremely uncomfortable in such closely intimate proximity to the other girl, Poppy stared in fascination as Suky let her towel drop, exposing a nest of black curls. Suky put her fingertips to them, revealing lips of pink flesh glistening with moisture. As Poppy stared she became aware that her heart was pounding. Her mouth had gone dry and she circled her lips with her tongue.

'This is my little button of joy,' Suky whispered excitedly, touching her clitoris. 'It feels lovely when I stroke it.' Poppy watched wide-eyed as Suky's fingertips flitted over the little bead of flesh, making it grow larger until it emerged from its hiding place impertinently, evidently eager for more. 'If I do this for long enough I'll come...'

'C-come?' Poppy's smooth brow furrowed as she tried to fathom out the myriad thoughts crashing around her head. 'How do you mean, exactly?'

'You know, I'll have a wonderful orgasm,' Suky teased huskily, her almond eyes holding Poppy's as she leaned closer, her small breasts brushing against Poppy's larger, still damp breasts. Suky's lips parted and the slightly older, spellbound girl saw her pink tongue moving behind her neat white teeth as she said, '*You* do it, Popsicle.'

Poppy had never been called by a pet name at the college before, and there was no denying Suky was very attractive, but her upbringing had made her wary of and uncomfortable with intimacy, particularly with another female, and she realised she was slowly shaking her head. 'N-no, Suky,' she heard herself bluster. 'I... I think we should get dressed now.'

Poppy escaped into the cubicle she'd used to change previously, the longing ever stronger between her thighs, and when she tentatively glanced over her shoulder the lovely dusky girl was standing with her back to her, her lustrous black hair hanging to her waist, but it was something else that made her catch her breath and stare; Suky's lovely buttocks were scored from side to side with livid welts, the marks of a severe chastisement!

Apart from the food on offer, lunch that day was a virtual repeat of breakfast, except that Captain Smythe was there - unlike breakfast, when he hadn't been.

Poppy glanced at him throughout the meal, and although to her eyes he was positively ancient, she found his greying hair and aura of authority almost attractive. The cloistered life at Maidenhall may have kept her ignorant of sex, but as she picked at her food she couldn't erase the memories of what had happened to her in that one amazing morning - the spanking from Miss Brady, Suky flirting with her in the pool changing rooms, and last but by no means least, the bizarre scene in the gym and her first ever sight of a penis... an erect penis!

'Cavendish!' Miss Brady's harsh tone made Poppy's heart miss a beat. 'You weren't trying to skip our counselling session, I hope? Into my office, *now!*'

Miss Brady led the uncertain girl to the polished mahogany door marked *Housemistress*, selected a key from the bunch on the chain around her stout waist, and snapped the lock open with a harsh, *click!* She then beckoned to Poppy in a way that brooked no argument, and the girl's knees turned to jelly as with a quaking heart she followed the teacher's formal black suit and sensible shoes into the panelled room, where Miss Brady closed the door and went to stand behind her desk.

'Well, Cavendish?' she said, her disdainful gaze travelling up from the girl's black shoes and white socks, lingered over her creamy thighs, on up to where her breasts smoothly filled the white shirt, the striped tie nestling neatly between them, and then settled sternly on her wide-eyed, fearful face. 'Why did you resist my punitive therapy this morning?' There was a heavy silence in the musty office, save for the ticking of a clock. 'Well? I'm waiting for an answer.'

'I'm... I'm sorry, miss.' Hanging her head in shame, Poppy joined her hands meekly in front of her. 'I-I don't really know why.'

Miss Brady seemed somewhat mollified by Poppy's humble manner as she took her by the hand and led her behind her desk.

'You're soon to go out into the harsh world outside these walls, Cavendish,' she stated, staring at the girl with uncompassionate eyes. 'You've absolutely no idea how the male species will take advantage of you if you're prepared to give in to the kind of licentiousness you were engaged in this morning.'

Poppy watched hopelessly as Miss Brady took the penalty book from her drawer and consulted it.

'Hmmm...' she pondered the open pages, 'that's now three black marks against your name since the start of last term. You do realise I could take this to Miss Sharpe and recommend expulsion, don't you?'

'No, miss!' Poppy couldn't stand the shame or injustice of such a threat. 'Expulsion? Please, anything but that!'

'Anything?' Miss Brady's expression became one of sly calculation.

'Yes miss, *anything* miss.'

'So you agree to accept any course of action I consider appropriate?'

'Yes miss, I do,' Poppy said honestly, without really thinking further than the predicament she was in at that precise moment. 'Whatever you consider appropriate, miss.'

With a sudden movement that took Poppy by complete shock and surprise the housemistress seized the girl's wrist, tugged it under the hem of her black skirt, and pressed it up tight against her sex mound, the skirt rucked up over the girl's disappearing forearm. Poppy's shocked senses had barely registered the feel of crisp pubic hair through cotton drawers when Miss Brady pushed her hand away again, hurried to the door and locked it with one of her chained keys, and turned back towards the mortified girl. With alarming haste she then tore her blouse open and advanced, her white breasts exposed and swaying from side to side.

Poppy's dry mouth dropped open in amazement as the older woman cupped the back of the girl's head with both hands and pulled her flushed face to her cavernous cleavage, and the girl was obeying a deep-rooted instinct as she caught a rubbery nipple between her lips and began to suck.

'At last you are acting more sensibly,' Miss Brady breathed, tight-lipped. 'Now lift your skirt, Cavendish.'

Excitement and confusion vied for prominence as Poppy obeyed instantly and lifted her pleated skirt submissively about her waist, and the battle intensified when Miss Brady grasped the tight elastic waist and tugged her navy-blue knickers down to mid-thigh. Then with the speechless teenager's naked buttocks and pubic nest exposed, the teacher ordered, 'And now, you will bend over my desk...'

Poppy hesitated only for a moment, and then her soft breasts, encased in her white shirt, flattened down onto the polished oak, and she waited timorously as Miss Brady plucked a wooden ruler from her desk-tidy, raised it menacingly into the air, and hissed sternly, 'I'd better not hear the slightest whimper from you, you troublesome little wretch!'

Thwack!

Poppy's bottom recoiled under the force of the blow, and as her toned flesh sprang back into perfect roundness she gasped at the searing pain. Yet when the housemistress's fingers touched her a moment later they opened first her pussy lips, and then probed her clitoral hood with the utmost tenderness. Poppy's hips moved instinctively, but then the fingers were gone again.

Thwack!

The ruler cut down a second time, and as Poppy rocked against the desk and cringed from the pain she knew that her tormentor had pulled her own skirt up, for she felt a bare knee and thigh rubbing between hers. Then something humid rubbed against the scalding weals that had risen across Poppy's punished buttocks, making her squirm with more ardent abandon.

Thwack!

Any simmering pleasure she may have felt was washed away on a fresh wave of pain, and this time, despite her determination and resolve, Poppy could not suppress an anguished whimper.

'Quiet, young lady!' Miss Brady hissed vehemently, giving no quarter or compassion.

Once again fingers touched Poppy intimately, and the wet sounds induced from between her trembling thighs made her blush with shame. As some fingers held her vaginal lips open another stimulated her clitoris, and Poppy's mouth fell open and her eyes closed, unable and unwilling to resist the climax that was approaching through her every nerve and sinew. Panting, she strained her hindquarters backwards and lifted her head to gaze dreamily over her shoulder, for some reason willing the formidable Miss Brady to look into her eyes. And the lecturer did, clearly saw the depth of her pupil's need, and with sadistic cruelty ceased her knowledgeable fingering of her.

Then, with her eyes locked on Poppy's, she raised the wooden implement and slashed it down.

Swish...!

13

It swatted so close to the girl's beaten buttocks that her eyes widened and her whole body tensed as she awaited the intense pain... that never came.

Several more times the strict woman cut the air behind her victim with the heavy ruler.

Swish...! Swish...! Swish...!

Each time Poppy's bottom, adorned now with broad, mottled bands where the instrument of correction had struck, squirmed with an exquisite mix of fear and pleasure as she listened to the cruel, tormenting sound. Then wanting to take her sport further, Miss Brady stepped out of her own cotton drawers, held their damp crotch in front of her student's eyes, and growled, 'You'll not make a sound this time...'

Having stuffed the pungent undergarment between Poppy's inert lips, filling her mouth, making her breathe through flared nostrils, she brought the ruler down harder than ever on her throbbing flesh.

Thwack!

If the pain of the strike was intense, so was the pleasure that followed as the housemistress's skilful fingers again sought out and stimulated Poppy's clitoris as her wet, hairy sex resumed its rubbing against her tormented buttocks, and although Miss Brady uttered not a sound, Poppy knew she was coming when she felt her body tremble, tense, and then shudder against her punished behind and thighs.

A few moments later, when her sexual spasms had gradually subsided, Miss Brady touched the girl's shoulder, and still bewildered by what had happened, she unquestioningly straightened up and turned around.

'Have you learned your lesson now, Cavendish?' Miss Brady drew her knickers from Poppy's mouth and smiled, showing a side to her personality that the girl had never seen before.

'Oh *yes*, miss,' Poppy sighed sincerely. 'You were right; I needed to be corrected. I do feel better for it... I think.'

Poppy's years at Maidenhall had been devoid of love, and she could not remember ever being embraced, nor had she ever expected to be. But although Miss Brady's lusts had been satisfied she stayed close, and for some inexplicable reason Poppy put her arms around the lecturer's waist and rested her cheek gratefully against her shoulder. The housemistress's blouse was still hanging open, her large breasts protruding, and it seemed natural that Poppy should tentatively touch her tongue-tip to a nipple and draw it into her mouth.

Miss Brady reached down and held both their skirts up in one hand, and used the other to first stroke Poppy's silky pubic hair, then to rub her own coarser curls. They remained like that, in comfortable silence, for two or three long minutes.

'What is it, Poppy?' the lecturer eventually asked, unusually using the girl's Christian name.

'I don't know, miss,' Poppy whispered. 'But I feel there should be something more.'

Miss Brady nodded understandingly, and guided Poppy gently back until her

14

tender buttocks touched the edge of the desktop. Then feeding her knickers back into the girl's mouth, she got down onto her knees before her and touched the insides of her thighs with her hands. When the girl's legs parted, voluntarily but somewhat uncertainly, the housemistress raised her fingers and parted her juicy vaginal lips.

The extreme gentleness of her tongue on Poppy's clitoris made the girl's nipples tingle madly, and she began her inexorable tumble into an explosive orgasm almost at once. Perhaps because she had been cheated of it on more than one occasion already that day, her first experience of a sexual climax was so intense that she was glad to be gagged with her lecturer's knickers so as not to alert anyone who might be passing by the office, but even so she moaned loudly through them...

As a key turned in the lock Miss Brady looked up, her mouth and chin glistening wetly with Poppy's fragrant juices. Her drawers still showed white between Poppy's parted lips, and the girl's eyes widened in alarm as the two of them froze and watched the doorknob slowly turn, and the door slowly open, creaking slightly on its tired old hinges.

Poppy wanted to curl up and die as Miss Sharpe and Captain Smythe appeared, and then she frantically grappled to remove the underwear from her mouth. Guilt was added to her cocktail of spiralling emotions when she realised it was probably her fault they had been found out, her moan of suppressed passion having given them away as the headmistress and the chairman of governors passed along the corridor outside the tiny office.

'What on *earth...?*' the headmistress blurted, having been speechless for several tense seconds, and then as she watched Miss Brady get up off her knees she thundered, 'Never in all my years of teaching have I seen *anything* such as this. *You!*' Her face a mask of outrage, she pointed a trembling finger at the housemistress. 'You're fired! Go to your quarters and pack immediately. I won't have you around my girls a moment longer!'

Then as Miss Brady slunk out, shamefaced, Miss Sharpe turned on Poppy. 'And as for you, Cavendish, you can go and wait outside the infirmary. You'll be lucky if your pursuit of unnatural love has not landed you on the streets by nightfall!'

Poppy risked a fearful glance at Captain Smythe as she slipped guiltily past him, trying to straighten her dishevelled clothing. The ex-army officer's blue eyes glinted as they took in her state of undress and his mouth, so used to delivering barked orders, was set in a grim, firm line.

Miss Sharpe lived on the ground floor of a two-storey house built against the college's redbrick perimeter wall, and the infirmary occupied the floor above. As Poppy crossed the deserted quadrangle she looked up at its expressionless windows and felt a greater sense of unease than any she had experienced so far, for it seemed from the headmistress's threat that her worst fear was about to be realised.

If only she could persuade them not to expel her, she thought in desperation, she'd agree to any punishment they proposed. The door to the infirmary was locked, and as Miss Sharpe did not appear for what seemed like an age, Poppy killed anxious time by gazing at the walls that loomed above her, shielding her from the outside world.

For the first time in her life she noticed a strange emblem on the clock tower where it abutted the college wall. Once gilt, now badly weathered, it depicted a medieval archer with his bow drawn and an arrow about to leave it, a logo that seemed oddly familiar. Poppy was wondering about this when a door in West House opened aggressively and Miss Sharpe stormed out. Oh no, the girl thought with growing apprehension, obviously Captain Smythe had given her a telling off for allowing such things to carry on in her college, and now she'd take it out on her!

The head teacher unlocked the infirmary door with a key fastened to her waist chain and pointed grimly to the steep staircase within.

'Up those stairs!' she ordered fiercely, and Poppy climbed the wooden staircase ahead of Miss Sharpe, ashamed because she knew the woman would be able to see up her skirt at her tight blue knickers.

When they reached the top the fearsome woman said, 'For the way you've behaved I'm putting you in the isolation room, Cavendish.' It was obvious that she thought Poppy should be treated as though she had a contagious disease as she propelled her into a small, windowless room that contained only a metal-framed bed fixed to one wall, a metal wardrobe and a basin, and said sternly, 'I am not having you mixing with the other girls and corrupting them with your salacious ways. Now, there are no day clothes allowed in the infirmary, so get undressed.'

'But, miss...' Poppy regarded Miss Sharpe fearfully, 'I have nothing else to wear.'

'You will strip to your underwear.' Miss Sharpe's countenance was one of intense anger as she wagged a warning finger at the observation window in one wall, which gave a clear view from the small infirmary next door. 'And if your disgusting, licentious nature tempts you to so much as put a hand inside your knickers, we'll know about it!'

She stormed out, slamming the door behind her and turning the key in the lock. The light switch was outside and before she marched away she flooded the room with bright light.

Left alone with her thoughts, Poppy lay down on the unwelcoming, institutional mattress. Surprisingly for Maidenhall, where thrift was the norm, the isolation room was very warm. She glanced inquisitively at the observation window, then lay on her back and gazed up at the cracks in the ceiling. Her mind drifted to the climax of her encounter with Miss Brady, and she wished she could touch herself as, despite her parlous predicament, her wicked excitement continued to simmer. Imagining lying in her narrow bed in the East House dormitory she wondered if she would ever go back there, and felt a strong sense of regret that she had not said a proper goodbye to Karen Stringfellow.

Hours passed, but though the main infirmary eventually grew dark the bright light inside the isolation room made sleep impossible, and in the end Poppy was simply unable to resist defying her headmistress, and began to touch herself. First she fingered her nipples through her bra, and then she parted her legs and rubbed herself through her panties. She pulled their elastic aside to allow the tentative entry of a finger, but as she was about to touch her fingertip to her clitoris, something made her glance at the observation window again, and to her horror she saw that two dark shapes were standing there, motionless, and she realised with a sinking heart that Captain Smythe and Miss Sharpe were watching her very closely.

Chapter 2

Flushed crimson with guilt and shame Poppy hastily clamped her legs together and snatched her finger from between them, only realising the window was soundproofed when she saw the silhouette of the couple talking to each other, probably discussing her fate.

Then they moved out of sight and were gone for a long, long time, and Poppy could do nothing but wait for them to return and deliver her sentence, and gradually, shielding her eyes from the glare of the light with her forearm, she fell into a fitful sleep.

It must have been very late at night when they returned, Miss Sharpe unlocking the door and flinging one of Poppy's freshly laundered uniforms onto the bed.

'Get dressed, Poppy Cavendish,' the headmistress commanded, and as Poppy rose and stood in her white bra and panties, she noticed that Captain Smythe was again at the observation window, staring at her in a way that made her feel extremely insecure. 'And when you're dressed,' the formidable woman went on, 'come through to the main infirmary. We have consulted, and decided what is to become of you.'

Hardly caring any more what they had decided, Poppy pulled on her white socks, buttoned the white shirt over her breasts and tucked it into her pleated skirt, which she fastened at one hip. She tied her tie neatly and bent to buckle her shoes, took a deep breath, and she was ready to face them, walking slowly into the next room.

'Cavendish, come over here.' Captain Smythe crooked a finger in her direction, and then inverted the straightened digit to point at the floor in front of him as he spoke to her directly for the first time. Remembering the humble manner that had placated Miss Brady earlier, Poppy moved to obey, with her hands joined meekly before her and her eyes cast respectfully downward. With military bearing he stuck out his chin, his face inches from hers. 'You've been a very naughty girl, haven't you?' he said.

'Um, yes sir,' Poppy responded humbly, knowing it was the sensible thing to do, 'I suppose I have.'

Captain Smythe glared at her so harshly that she cringed under the severity of the look, then in a tone that demanded an immediate response he demanded, 'A *dirty* girl?'

'Um, yes sir,' Poppy replied, not really sure of his point, what he was getting at.

'I can't hear you.'

'I said yes, sir, I've been a dirty girl.'

Captain Smythe nodded pensively. 'Well then, there are two courses of action open to us.' He frowned and indicated a trunk on the floor. It was Poppy's trunk. Its lid was open and Poppy saw her meagre possessions inside. 'We've packed your things for you,' he went on. 'In my opinion you should leave this college forthwith, tonight.' The summer weather had turned and a gust of wind sent rain lashing against the darkened windows, and Poppy shivered although the infirmary was warm enough. 'But very fortunately for you,' he continued, 'Miss Sharpe has a more compassionate nature than me. She interceded on your behalf and asked that I administer more tried and tested methods of discipline, those which the do-gooders have banned in their misguided way.'

Pausing impressively he glared at the miserable girl, and as she cringed, unable to meet his stare, he said menacingly, 'In other words, that I administer a sound thrashing...'

He paused again dramatically to allow his words to sink in, and then went on. 'If you agree to this we will keep our promise and find you a position of employment outside. Now, what is it to be?'

Poppy considered her meagre options for a moment. 'Please sir,' she eventually said, looking up at him with pleading eyes, 'I will accept the physical punishment.'

At that moment she wished only to humble herself to the captain's will, her acquiescence making her aware, perhaps for the first time, of her own innate wish to serve. With this dawning realisation of her inner desire to subjugate herself to the will of others, there came a return of that tantalising, insistent tingling between her legs.

Captain Smythe nodded curtly and turned to Miss Sharpe. 'I think a severe spanking should do this time,' he said. 'Do you agree, headmistress?'

'So long as it *is* severe, captain.' There was no disguising the doubt in Miss Sharpe's voice.

'It will be, never fear, dear lady,' Captain Smythe said with a harshness that made Poppy's heartbeat quicken.

'If you sit on this, captain,' Miss Sharpe said, positioning a straight-backed chair for him, 'you can put her precisely over your knee.' She looked sternly at Poppy, shook her head with an expression of disappointment and said tersely, 'It's time you learned the error of your ways, young lady.'

To her eternal shame, Poppy was unable to repress a pleasurable shudder as Captain Smythe sat and guided her facedown over his thighs. She remembered Miss Brady's stimulation of her clitoris earlier, imagined the captain's stout fingers circling the little organ, and wondered if he'd touch her intimately too.

This made a sensation pulse between her legs that reached all the way up to her nipples, but the force with which he gripped the back of her neck and pushed her head towards the floor was unsettling, and drove all thoughts of illicit pleasure from her mind.

As she stared in shock at his highly polished shoes and his expensive cavalry twills, Captain Smythe's right leg lifted over the back of her shapely thighs and trapped them there. Pinioned and completely helpless she lay vanquished by his will, unable to move. Again she became aware of her heart pounding and felt an overwhelming need to be free, yet even as she drew breath convulsively she was aware that part of her revelled in her loss of control, that she had always longed for a feeling just like this.

Captain Smythe lifted his free hand, which had been lying companionably across the backs of her thighs.

'Her skirt's protecting her,' he said.

'Yes, it is,' Miss Sharpe agreed, and Poppy felt the headmistress's hands lift her skirt by its hem and fold it onto her back, and she tensed her panty-clad buttocks against the blow she was sure would immediately follow. But to her surprise she felt Captain Smythe's hand moving with surprising gentleness over the roundness of her bottom, one of his fingers even taking the liberty of tracing the line of her perennial divide.

Smack!

The blow, when it came, was of such force Poppy gasped and rocked forward on his lap, and then held her breath against the searing pain as it crept up on her.

Smack!

His seasoned palm swept down again across her buttocks, flattening the fleshy rounds momentarily. Poppy gasped again, there was a momentary pause, and then he delivered a volley of severe spanks, as he'd vowed to Miss Sharpe, her skin reddened beneath her uniform knickers, her creamy thighs parted very slightly - a reaction not missed by the punisher and his accomplice - and she ground her hips against his lap in an instinctive but hopelessly futile attempt to distance herself from the pain.

'Be careful, captain,' Miss Sharpe warned. 'I doubt she's above trying to satisfy her depraved appetite in any way possible.'

'You have many sinful instincts, young lady,' Captain Smythe growled, and then with an air of righteous indignation, he raised his hand again and brought it down in a veritable fusillade of blows. Then with his own palm beginning to sting from the force of the smacks delivered, the captain reasserted his vicelike grip on the back of her neck and diverted his concentration to the backs of her silken thighs, targeting the gorgeous girl there instead.

'Oh, *sir*,' she sobbed, 'please, no more...'

Rather surprisingly the spanking did actually stop then, but as Poppy lay over his lap, breathing heavily after the punishment, she was disturbed to feel Captain Smythe's hand caressing over her knickers. At the same time she became conscious of a lump pressing up into her lower tummy. She remembered the rigid thrust of the male organ she'd spied that morning, and wondered if it had actually belonged to Captain Smythe. Who else could it have been?

And had the matronly woman been none other than Miss Sharpe?

And was the hapless girl bound to the wall-bars Suky? That would certainly explain the welts she'd seen adorning her bottom in the swimming pool changing rooms.

Despite her awful situation, Poppy felt a knot of excitement in the area of her body where the lump pressed, and her shamefully lascivious response was to gently writhe against it. To do so felt good, and the swelling grew both bigger and firmer in response. With tears glistening in her lashes as her hair swept the polished tiled floor, Poppy surreptitiously nibbled her lip as her secret pleasure increased.

'Well, well, Miss Sharpe,' the overbearing man said, Poppy cringing as she realised her movements had been detected, 'the young lady appears to be deriving pleasure from this even as we punish her.'

'We're too soft on them, Captain Smythe, that's our trouble,' the headmistress said. 'Far too soft by half. I believe it's time we got tougher with the girls, starting right now with this little trollop. It's for their own good, after all.'

So saying, the headmistress hooked her fingers into the elastic of Poppy's tight knickers and pulled them down almost to her knees. The girl's bare, peach-like buttocks were revealed in all their mouth-watering glory, blotched red with the palm prints that Captain Smythe's spanking had produced. But underlying these, and visible only at their edges, were traces of broad stripes that diverted Miss Sharpe from the task in hand. Exchanging a wordless glance with the captain, she traced the welts inquisitively with her fingertips. 'Did Miss Brady punish you?' she asked directly.

'Yes, miss,' Poppy admitted, her natural honesty coming to the fore before she'd even thought about her response. 'She said I needed some form of correction.'

Miss Sharpe did not respond visibly to this disclosure.

'I agree with you wholeheartedly, Miss Sharpe,' the captain said, concurring with her previous opinion. 'And I believe you have preserved a particular instrument of correction from more enlightened times?'

'I have indeed, sir, yes.'

'Good. Then please bring it to me, if you would be so kind.'

As Miss Sharpe crossed to where locked, glass-fronted cabinets gleamed with rows of brightly shining surgical instruments, Poppy was surprised to feel a hand squeeze under her body, and with a heart-stopping sense of anticipation she thought he was going to touch her where he shouldn't. The hand rummaged, Poppy felt and heard his zip being opened, and while the headmistress went through her bunch of keys he lifted the girl very slightly, and the lump pulsed minutely against her now naked lower tummy, the bulbous tip of it actually nestling in her soft pubic hair!

'This is what you mean, I believe.' The headmistress cut the air with a thin, flexible cane she'd lifted reverently from a tall jar on one of the shelves. 'I've had it soaking in vinegar for just such an occasion as this.'

'Many thanks, headmistress,' he said. 'That looks just perfect.' He took it, and the cane was no sooner in his hand than he cut the air with an ominous sound that made Poppy's buttocks clench as fear gripped her. 'Remove her knickers for me, if you please.'

Poppy lay meekly over his lap, the column of warm flesh pulsing secretly close to the apex of her thighs, as the woman pulled her knickers down her legs and over her shoes and socks.

There was a tense pause, an unsettling silence falling over the room, and then Poppy was submerged in an ocean of pain as Captain Smythe scored her bare bottom with stripe after cruel stripe with the cane, his actions causing his body - and in particular his groin - to rub ever more insistently and rhythmically against the delicious writhing girl, until he was forced to abruptly curtail the caning.

'Ahem, Miss Sharpe,' he said, his tone tight as he held out the instrument of correction. 'Would you care to complete the punishment for me?'

'Off course I would, captain, gladly.' Eyes gleaming with zeal, the woman raised the cane high and rained blow after blow on Poppy's already striped and tormented flesh. The girl managed to turn and lift her head and looked up tearfully at the captain's ruddy face, and she was alarmed by the glazed expression in his eyes, the way his lips set in a firm line of determination, and as the captain's penis lurched between her thighs Poppy could not suppress a cry of mingled pain and shameful pleasure.

'Strumpet,' the captain grunted, the insult making the innocent Poppy sob afresh as he added ominously, 'you are mine, and will remain so forever, no matter whose bed I may send you to.' Then he tensed and closed his eyes, and Poppy felt his erection lurch again and a warm, viscous spillage seep into her pubic curls and coat her tummy.

'That's enough,' Captain Smythe eventually decreed, sounding weary. 'Get up and return to the observation room, Cavendish. You'll need to get a good night's sleep in readiness for some big changes to your life in the days to come.'

Chastised and chastened, Poppy rose stiffly and picked up her knickers, cringing as the cooling semen soaked into her skirt, and as the soft material agitated her beaten buttocks. The severity of the punishment that agonised Poppy's poor bottom had already begun moulding her to their will, and she obediently went through to the small room she'd occupied previously.

'You owned up to your wickedness, Cavendish,' Captain Smythe said, standing in the open doorway, Miss Sharpe behind him and just to his side, 'and taken your punishment bravely.' His brooding eyes scrutinised hers without pity. 'In return, I will honour my pledge and find you a suitable position elsewhere.'

Without another word they retreated and Miss Sharpe closed the door and locked it, and a moment later Poppy heard their footsteps fading as they went down the stairs and into Miss Sharpe's living quarters below.

Poppy undressed again and got into the uncomfortable bed, just in time, for the light suddenly went out. After a few minutes the throbbing in her punished buttocks became too much, so she turned over to lie on her tummy. Events had happened so thick and fast since that morning that she really was exhausted, and too tired for any meaningful thoughts. Sleep stole over her quickly.

Poor Poppy was so naïve, unschooled as yet in the guile and intent of predatory seducers. It never occurred to her that events might have been arranged, that her responses had been monitored, her behaviour cynically manipulated. The lovely girl fell into an innocent sleep with not even a glimmer that she might be a mere puppet, a beautiful marionette dancing to the sexual rhythm of others.

Chapter 3

The clock tower bell tolled, dragging Poppy from a troubled sleep that was filled with sexual imagery and snatches of portentous conversations. As she stretched and rolled over the discomfort in her buttocks made her wince and brought her to the present with a jolt.

She sat up tentatively, relieved to discover the pain of the previous day and night's punishments had mellowed to a relatively pleasant, pulsing warmth. Her memory of Captain Smythe's furious chastisement became linked in her mind to her dreams, some of which had again involved Karen Stringfellow. As the jigsaw pieces fell spiralling into her mind she thought that perhaps the captain was right - she was a strumpet.

In one dream Poppy was in the dormitory in East House and found Karen lying facedown on her bed, wearing only her hockey socks. Her single plait of golden hair lay down her back, and Poppy was shocked to see that her buttocks were striped with angry ridges of pain, the signature of an intense chastisement. She sat on the edge of the bed and pressed her cool hands to the welted flesh, and Karen moved her legs so that her thighs were slightly parted. She looked over her shoulder, and her eyes had held Poppy's in a strange, hypnotic gaze as she placed her fingers over Poppy's and used their tips to pull her buttocks apart.

The conscious Poppy remembered the way the pale rosebud of her friend's anus became exposed, and how the little minx penetrated the tight aperture with one finger as far as the first knuckle. She rolled her hips invitingly back and forth, and her tongue flitted behind the whiteness of her neat teeth, but when she spoke it was in the husky voice of Suky Desai. 'You do it for me, Popsicle,' she urged. '*You* do it.'

Poppy had reached out slowly, extending her middle finger with the intention of using it to trace the neat, moist ring of Karen's rear hole, but as soon as she touched it she had climaxed in her sleep.

Ashamed now of her nocturnal ardour, she swung her legs out from beneath the sheets and sat on the edge of the bed, trying to clear her head.

Was the confrontational conversation between Captain Smythe and Miss Sharpe part of her dream, too? She was sure she remembered Miss Sharpe storming, 'I can't believe you've done it again! What if she tells them? We'll be ruined!'

Captain Smythe countered aggressively, to which Miss Sharpe snapped, 'And just who will have to sort it all out? Me, as usual!' Or was she imagining the whole thing?

Poppy could catch no more elusive threads of memory, and as she tried to separate dreams from reality a key turned without warning in the locked door, which then opened.

'Good morning.' Miss Sharpe entered the room bearing a breakfast tray, her usually stern expression relaxed in a partial smile. The headmistress put the tray down and handed Poppy a regulation linen nightdress. To the girl's immense surprise, she then perched her large bottom precariously on the side of the bed and watched her in silence.

Poppy half turned away to slip the nightdress on, uncomfortably conscious of Miss Sharpe's eyes on her breasts, which quivered firmly as she raised her arms to allow the nightdress over her head. Then picking up the bowl of cereal she cast furtive glances at the woman, wondering what she was up to. A change had come over her; her hair had been set free from its usual tight bun, and she looked far less fearsome than usual. Poppy detected the outline of her nipples through her blouse, and suspected the austere woman was not wearing a bra.

When she'd finished the cereal, she summoned the courage to ask the question that was uppermost in her mind.

'Any news of my position of employment, miss?'

'Well, you cannot start in your post until you are one hundred percent fit,' the woman told her.

Poppy grimaced prettily. 'My bottom is somewhat sore, miss, if that's what you mean.'

'You'd better let me take a look at it.' Miss Sharpe bustled about finding antiseptic cream and a healing unguent. 'Lift your nightgown,' she instructed, 'and lie facedown on the bed.'

Poppy obeyed and Miss Sharpe's decisive hands were soon moving over her marked buttocks in a circular motion that was soothing and soporific. The prone girl almost dozed off when the headmistress inadvertently touched a particularly harsh welt, casing Poppy to jump and wince. 'Ouch,' she gasped.

The woman paused, waiting for Poppy to relax again, then she dipped her fingers in fragrant oil and resumed the hypnotic caress, gradually slipping into the shadowy valley dividing the luscious buttocks, circling the tiny aperture there with a tenderness that surprised the student and made her clitoris tingle luxuriously.

'Oh, miss...' Poppy began to slowly rotate her hips in response to the gentle probing of the finger. 'Oh... oh... oh...' she murmured, and then to her disappointment Miss Sharpe straightened up and moved away from the bed.

'That's you done, Cavendish,' she said, her ascetic manner re-established. 'I'll see you at lunch.' And then she was gone, the door shut again, and Poppy heard the key turning in the lock, filled with bewilderment and confused emotions of embarrassment and disappointment.

'Oh, dear.' She had thought for a moment that Miss Sharpe was going to enact some of the things Karen Stringfellow had done in her dream, but now she felt unwanted and alone again.

The headmistress delivered a typically institutional lunch of liver, boiled potatoes and cabbage. But Poppy barely touched it, so distracted was she by the presence of the woman, and concerns over her future. She wanted to ask what was planned for her, but dared not because she didn't want to risk incurring the wrath of the woman, and because she wasn't sure she wanted to hear the answer - even if she received one.

Miss Sharpe took the tray with the remains of the partly eaten meal from the girl, and Poppy was just reconciling herself to coping with another period of loneliness, when the woman, having taken the tray out into the infirmary, returned and determinedly closed the door.

She stood in front of Poppy, where the girl sat on the edge of the bed, then without a word of explanation she began to methodically unbutton her blouse, staring intently at the girl's beautiful, spellbound face, her mouth hanging open in amazement. When the blouse was open she pulled it from the waistband of her tweed skirt, exposing her large breasts to the stunned gaze of the girl.

Poppy could not believe what was now happening.

'I shouldn't be doing this, Cavendish,' the woman said very matter-of-factly. 'Captain Smythe would be extremely angry if he knew.'

'N-no, miss...' Poppy blurted, her mind in a spin. 'I - I mean yes, miss...'

The headmistress weighed one heavy breast, and cupping the back of Poppy's head with her free hand, fed a stiff nipple between the mesmerised girl's lips, and perhaps because she had been starved of any maternal love, the girl sucked hungrily, murmuring as she did so. She stared trustingly up into Miss Sharpe's eyes as they looked down into hers, and when Poppy's lips left the woman's breast, leaving its nipple glistening wet, the headmistress took her face in both hands and bent to kiss her passionately.

It was Poppy's first amorous kiss, and she was unprepared for the tongue that probed her mouth, but after an initial reluctance to accept it she soon found the experience immensely enjoyable. And when her own tongue tentatively responded it was immediately sucked into the headmistress's mouth.

Then after the long kiss Miss Sharpe bent to lift the hem of Poppy's nightgown and pulled it over her head.

'Is your bottom still sore, Cavendish?' she asked, guiding Poppy up to her feet, and her hands stroked lightly over the girl's uncomfortable buttocks with unbearable tenderness, then touched her pussy fleetingly. Poppy's wide eyes stared into the headmistress's as she nodded, lost for words. 'Then I'll be gentle with you. Lie down and turn onto your front.'

Poppy obeyed and Miss Sharpe bent to whisper in her ear, 'Sometimes the body's natural remedies are the best, Cavendish. I'm going to sooth your bottom with something very, very special. Don't be alarmed.'

As Poppy held her breath and waited to see what she was going to do, the headmistress climbed onto the bed and straddled the shapely form lying quietly, and Miss Sharpe's sex moved on her welted buttocks in a slow, circular motion, making wet sounds from time to time.

The girl groaned into the pillow with gathering excitement as hands squeezed beneath her, first to maul her breasts and roll her nipples between fingers and thumbs, and then to move down and invade the wetness between her legs and stimulate the flesh that nestled there. Helpless beneath the headmistress's robust body, she felt strangely safe and secure.

Their mutually mounting excitement was punctuated with moans, gasps and groans, until Poppy felt Miss Sharpe's wet sex pressing desperately against her sore buttocks as she shuddered through an intense and dizzying orgasm above her. This triggered her own climax, and it was some time before their whimpers died away and they lay, utterly drained, together on the bed.

Thereafter Miss Sharpe brought her own meals to the infirmary and ate with Poppy, after which she would massage healing cream into the girl's tender flesh. Often they ended up in bed together, Poppy lying on her back sucking Miss Sharpe's breasts while the mature woman's stout form heaved above her. A few days passed, and Poppy's bottom healed nicely.

When the only sign that remained of her punishment were a few faint marks left by the cane, Miss Sharpe went to her quarters. She sat for a long time, staring at the old-fashioned telephone that sat on her desk like a squat, sinister black toad. She surprised even herself by how fond she had grown of Poppy Cavendish, and the enormity of the betrayal she was about to commit made her heart heavy as she lifted the receiver. When she had made the fateful telephone call she went back up to the infirmary with the announcement that would change Poppy's life forever.

'It's the captain's orders; you've to pack your trunk,' Miss Sharpe told the girl. 'He's found you a post as personal assistant to Sir Neville and Lady Bradburn.' Poppy wondered why the headmistress's mouth tightened as she added, 'They'll want to train you to their own specifications. Be sure to obey them in every way.'

'W-when do I go, miss?' the girl asked, her mouth dry with anxiety.

'Captain Smythe is picking us up in an hour.'

An *hour?*

Poppy noticed Miss Sharpe looking at her with something that looked like sympathy as they crossed the sunny quadrant to East House, where she was taken upstairs and locked in her old dormitory. Her trunk was on top of her locker and when she opened it her first thought was to wonder why one of her old college uniforms was inside. Surely it would be of absolutely no use to her or anybody now she was to leave the college for good.

Deciding it must be another example of Miss Sharpe's thrifty ways she packed it nevertheless, like the dutiful girl she was. Then as she struggled to close the lid on her dowdy wardrobe, a carved figure inside it caught her eye.

'That's funny,' she mused. It portrayed a medieval archer holding a bow and arrow, and when Poppy scraped below it with her nail she saw that a name had been painted over. *Major Charles Bowman*, she read, *22nd King's Hussars.* 'How strange,' she said to the empty room, 'it's the same design as on the clock tower...'

She supposed that the Maidenhall estate must have been owned by a family called Bowman at one time, and put the matter from her mind.

Although the college regime had been harsh, Poppy felt weepy now that she was about to leave. She lay on Karen Stringfellow's bed, recalled her frequent dreams and fantasies about her American friend, and not wanting to leave without saying goodbye to her, she quickly wrote her a note.

Dear Karen,

I'd need pages and pages to tell you about all the things that have happened since you left for your holidays. I'll tell you more about it all when next we meet.

Captain Smythe, of the board of governors, and Old Sharpie, who turns out not to be quite the fierce old bat we thought, have found me a post as a personal assistant to a couple in Burchester.

Let's write to each other, via the post office in Maidenhall village, poste restante. I'll find a way to post and collect letters if you'll do the same.

Love, Poppy

She slipped the note under Karen's pillow, where she would be sure to find it when she returned from her holidays, just as the headmistress opened the dormitory door and told Poppy it was time to be off.

As they walked down to the main hall carrying the trunk between them, Miss Sharpe spoke, apparently uncomfortable with what she wanted to say.

'Poppy...' she said, using solely the girl's Christian name for the first time ever. 'Yes, miss?'

'I, well, let's just say, I hope I can count on you to be discreet...'

Poppy remembered the weird verbal confrontation between the headmistress and Captain Smythe after they'd punished her, and still couldn't be sure if it was part of a dream or not. And of course the intimate things they'd been up to together since then came to the forefront of her mind, but her expression gave no indication of these thoughts and she met Miss Sharpe's strangely insecure look with an air of innocence as she asked, 'How do you mean, miss?'

A blush crept up Miss Sharpe's throat to her cheeks. In part of her thinking the college's staunchly moralistic foundations - and the rules, and the threat of scandal - must have remained strong because, in spite of all they had done together, sex was never mentioned directly. 'You must never breathe a word of what we've been doing together here, Poppy,' she said. 'Or that we used the methods that we did to punish you. Some people would not understand.'

'Yes miss, I think I know what you're saying. I won't say anything to anyone.' As Poppy spoke sincerely and the headmistress visibly relaxed, they both heard the purr of an engine and the crunch of tyres on gravel outside. Captain Smythe had arrived.

The two stared at each other as his confident footsteps marched up to the building, and when the large front door opened and he strode in, slapping his thigh with brown leather gloves as though with a riding crop, Poppy went a little weak at the knees.

This was it.

After years as an orphan being looked after by the institution that was Maidenhall, she was about to leave for good, to venture out into the world knowing she could not return to the protective walls that had surrounded her for so long if things didn't go well.

'Good morning, Cavendish,' he said, and then indicated her bottom with an imperious jerk of his chin. 'The marks on your rear have cleared up now?'

'Yes, sir.' As was usual, Poppy could not help feeling a little intimidated in his presence.

'Hmm.' The captain looked thoughtful. 'Perhaps I should take a look.'

'I think not,' Miss Sharpe said firmly.

Captain Smythe followed them as they struggled to his Daimler with Poppy's trunk, and unlocked the boot as though doing them a tremendous courtesy. Poppy sat alone on the back seat with her mentors in front.

It was a beautiful Saturday morning, and Poppy knew the few girls who had remained at Maidenhall for the summer would have taken advantage of the chance to go into the village, but she looked around out of the rear window in the futile hope of seeing the familiar face of at least one of her fellow students, just someone to wave goodbye to, but there was no one, and then before the captain could start the engine they heard the telephone ringing inside Miss Sharpe's living quarters across the quadrant. She climbed grumpily out of the car and went to answer it, and came back a minute later looking even more annoyed.

'Oh bother,' she said, 'this is so inconvenient. That was the lodge.' The lodge was the staff quarters where the teachers lived during term time. 'Apparently there's someone there from the electricity company. They need to have the meter cupboard opened, or something.'

As she lifted the large bunch of keys chained around her waist and selected the one she needed to let the meter reader in, the captain gave her a dismissive wave. 'By all means go and attend to it,' he said. 'We'll wait here.'

For some reason Miss Sharpe looked uneasy as she closed the car door on the passenger side and headed off in the direction of the lodge. Poppy felt uncomfortable at being left alone with the man, especially as he was so domineering and because of what they'd already done in the infirmary, and to make her disquiet even more intense she noticed him staring at her in the rear-view mirror.

'Come here, get in the front, Cavendish,' he said affably. 'I'll show you how to work the gear stick. You'll need to learn to drive now you're leaving here, and a quick lesson now will help no end.'

Not at all sure this was such a good idea, Poppy nonetheless obeyed, got out of the car and got back in beside him, blushing madly. Without a word he stared at her piercingly and placed her hand on the gear stick's round knob and covered it with his own. She was unable to meet his gaze and instead gazed down at the foot-well.

'First... second... third... fourth...' he instructed, moving her hand through the gears. 'And this...' he went on slyly, 'is fifth, Cavendish.'

He took her hand from the gear stick, and placed it over the evident swelling within his tweed trousers. Then staring into her wide eyes so intensely that she had to look away, he opened his trousers with his free hand, rummaged inside for a moment, shifting slightly in his seat to ease the task in hand, pulled out his erect penis, wrapped her inert fingers around the pulsing stalk, and began to move her hand up and down, up and down, until she found herself performing the act without his guidance as he lifted both his hands to maul her breasts through her shirt.

The moment Poppy saw Captain Smythe's erect cock, she knew it was the same one she'd seen through the knothole on the East House stairs. She was equally sure now that the female accomplice had been none other than Miss Sharpe, while the girl whose bottom they had taken turns to beat with the heavy belt was Suky Desai. Poppy's mouth went dry and her heartbeat increased as she realised for the first time that she was being drawn into a web of sexual intrigue. She ran her tongue over her lips to moisten them, an impulsive reaction that the captain immediately misinterpreted.

'I know exactly what you want, Cavendish,' he said, his voice husky, his moustache seeming to twitch a little. He glanced down at his cock, sprouting up from his lap, up from the opening in his tweeds, the bulbous head bloated and shiny, and smiled at her in the most carnal of leers. 'And you'll get what you want in a minute, but first I want to see *these*.'

Before Poppy could do or say anything more, he tugged her shirt out of the waistband of her skirt, put his hands up inside and dragged her bra down. In no time her shirt was undone, the two sides pulled apart, and her breasts were exposed to his lusty ogling as he cupped and squeezed them, groaning victoriously as though he was holding the eighth wonder of the world in his hands.

'Oh, *sir*...' she cried. 'Please, you shouldn't be doing this... *we* shouldn't be doing this. Miss Sharpe might come back at any moment?'

'Be quiet, girl,' he snapped, grinding his hips to enhance the sensations caused by her pumping fist, which continued to move up and down despite her fretting about what they were doing, fearful that someone might pass by and catch them.

But the captain seemed utterly unperturbed by such incidentals, and his hands continued to molest her exposed breasts with greedy insistence, pinching her nipples in a way that made her clitoris tingle shamefully. 'Normally I'd give you a spanking to warm you up, but as you say, Sharpe might return soon, so let's cut to the chase, eh?' And with that the man grabbed the nape of Poppy's neck in his usual vicelike grip and pressed her face down until it was inches from his sprouting cock. 'Come on, into your mouth with it,' he insisted.

Poppy's emotions were tumbling. Captain Smythe's attentions were making her clitoris pulse a sexual rhythm through her entire system, but although her pussy was brimming with juice at the excitement of again being so close to a male organ, the enormity of what he was demanding repulsed her. The tiny opening slit at the tip of his penis oozed a little drop of translucent liquid, and the thought of taking it into her mouth horrified her.

'Mm!' She transmitted her reluctance to do what he wanted through lips that were tightly sealed, at the same time trying to shake her head against the tight grip on her neck. 'Mm-mmmmm!'

'You little strumpet,' he growled. 'You little tease. You lead me on and then you get all coy. You think you can change your mind now? You're behaving like a spoilt little prick-teaser!'

His harsh diatribe stung Poppy, and the added persuasion of a spitefully pinched nipple convinced her to open her mouth just as the clamp on the back of her neck pressed. His cock touched her lips, eased them wider apart, and then surged on upward to fill her mouth, the smooth helmet actually touching the back of her throat, the tip of her nose and her chin touching his coarse tweed trousers, and to Poppy's immeasurable surprise a blissful feeling of surrender overwhelmed her.

She almost gagged involuntarily, but felt more satisfied and fulfilled than she ever remembered feeling in her life before. The captain's erection was so deeply embedded in her mouth that she could feel the wiry hairs at its base touching her lips, and she realised that by submitting totally to the man, to this cock, she could abdicate all will, be free of all responsibility, perhaps even lose her individuality and sense of self. The emotional counterpart to her need to submit was a feeling of overwhelming joy, and she felt a rush of exquisite sensations in her pussy that almost plunged her into an explosive orgasm.

'I could grow to quite like you, Cavendish, you little minx,' the captain grunted, holding her head with both hands and guiding it up and down in his lap, the gentle sound of her sucking the only other noise in the car. 'A bashful virgin one minute, and a deep-throating little strumpet the next.'

His cock-head lodged right in the back of her mouth, and Poppy could feel the muscles of his thighs alternately tensing and relaxing as he fought to control himself and maximise his pleasure.

'Up and down,' he instructed, 'and move your tongue against the underside at the same time. Oh yes, that's very good.' He began to grunt in unison with her inexperienced sucking, thrusting his hips in time with the exploratory movements of her head. 'Come on,' he urged gruffly. 'Come on, Sharpe may be back at any moment!'

His coarse, selfish encouragement - not to mention the throbbing column of flesh stretching her lips apart - had an amazing effect on Poppy, and she squeezed her thighs together to increase the pleasure being fuelled by the shameful situation she found herself in. Noticing this, Captain Smythe tugged her skirt up around her waist and managed to ease both hands into her knickers, one at the front and the other at the back, smiling slyly when her ministrations to his cock carried on instinctively even though he had released the grip on her head. As his right forefinger located her clitoris and toyed with it expertly, Poppy felt her orgasm begin its unstoppable ascent. Oh no, she thought, moving her hips desperately to allow him easier access between her thighs, she was going to come! And when another finger insinuated itself into the valley between her buttocks, sought out her little anal opening and rubbed around and around it, she knew that all hope was lost and tumbled into her most exhilarating orgasm yet. As her mind and body were washed in a wave of sexual ecstasy she almost recoiled when the captain swore vehemently, stiffened all over, and her mouth filled with spurt after spurt of warm, creamy semen, which she intuitively swallowed, knowing the only other alternative open for her was to risk incurring his wrath by making a mess of his trousers if she didn't.

'Get in the back, Cavendish,' he said abruptly, already tucking his wet and wilting penis into his trousers and straightening his clothes, and then bundling the bemused girl through the gap between the Daimler's front seats.

By the time Miss Sharpe returned and opened the front passenger car door the pair of them were sitting in formal silence, Captain Smythe in the front tapping the steering wheel and looking impatient, and Poppy in the back sitting primly with her hands in her lap and her knees together looking flushed.

'There was nobody there,' the woman said, eyeing them both suspiciously.

'Oh well,' Captain Smythe said blandly. 'Shall we press on?'

Moments later the Daimler was purring out of the college drive, and soon afterwards it whispered through Maidenhall village and passed the post office, the sight of it making Poppy think of Karen Stringfellow and bringing back her sense of loneliness.

As they stopped to let a tractor trundle by a young man sitting outside *The Bowman's Arms* looked over at them. He was quite handsome, with dark curly hair, and Poppy was amazed when he actually stood up and started moving towards them, staring at her strangely, and she was glad of the closed car window protecting her from the weirdo. As he reached them the road became clear and the car started moving again, and Poppy stared briefly into his eyes as he actually ran beside the vehicle, pointing at her.

'Listen to me!' she heard faintly through the thick glass. 'You must listen to me!'

Poppy was hugely unsettled by the strange encounter, but Captain Smythe drove on quickly, the fact that he did not want her to have any contact with the youth obvious, and his next words made the reason for this apparently clear.

'That's Jeff Riley, one of our local hoodlums, Cavendish,' he said without turning round or taking his eyes off the road. 'His family makes its living from that disreputable slum of a pub.'

The rest of the journey passed without incident and with little conversation between the headmistress and the chairman of the college governors, let alone between them and the girl sitting respectfully in the back. Poppy gazed silently out of the car windows as they drove through the countryside, and it was not too long before they reached the town of Burchester's outskirts, an area called Snode.

They passed a street sign, *Burr Crescent*, and drew up outside a large rambling house with a silver Mercedes parked outside. As they pulled into the drive a man wearing a chauffeur's livery came up from the basement and drove the silver limousine away, allowing Captain Smythe to take its place.

Miss Sharpe helped Poppy to carry her trunk up the front steps, and when the woman turned to face her, Poppy was surprised to see doubt etched into her face.

'Remember, Poppy,' she said conspiratorially, reaching across to squeeze her hand reassuringly. 'Do not tell them *anything*.'

And then Miss Sharpe rang the doorbell and retreated to the Daimler, which drove away without any other words being spoken to her... no goodbyes, nothing.

Poppy waited nervously before the large front door for what seemed a very long time, wondering if she should ring the bell again but wary of doing so.

Eventually a housemaid dressed in a traditional black uniform topped by a lacy white cap opened the door. The girl was pretty with dark shoulder-length hair and plump breasts encased smoothly within the black dress, the bib of her little white apron emphasising their pleasing shape. Poppy was disconcerted to find she was staring at the maid's attractive figure, and hastily lifted her gaze to her equally attractive face.

'I'm, um, Poppy Cavendish,' she introduced herself, although the housemaid's inexplicably hostile stare added to her confusion whilst standing, literally, on the threshold of a new life. 'I'm... I'm here to see Sir Neville and Lady Bradburn.'

'I know who you are,' the maid said abruptly, and then turning her back in a somewhat haughty manner, she added over her shoulder, 'You'd better follow me. Come on.'

They passed along a spacious hallway, and Poppy could hear voices drifting through an open door ahead. When the maid tut-tutted in annoyance and bent to pick up a minuscule piece of fluff from the carpet, the back of her skirt lifted and Poppy found herself staring at a neat bottom encased snugly in black silky knickers, but it was not the embarrassment of finding herself looking at another girl's bottom that made Poppy's heart clutch; it was the fading stripes she spied peeping out from her underwear and adorning the backs of her shapely thighs down to the tops of her black stockings.

What kind of a place, Poppy wondered as an icy fist of apprehension gripped her, had she been delivered to? But she also had to try to ignore the thrill that pulsed between her own thighs as the maid straightened up, led her into a drawing room and announced, 'Poppy Cavendish is here, sir and ma'am.'

An older woman stood up, extended her hand, and said benignly, 'Hello, I'm Lady Bradburn, and this is Sir Neville.' She indicated the distinguished looking gentleman drinking coffee opposite her, and shook hands with Poppy briskly, but the moment they broke contact her eyes hardened. 'You will address us as *sir* and *ma'am*,' she said. 'Now, let me hear you do so.'

'Good afternoon, ma'am,' Poppy said, and even bobbed a curtsy. 'Good afternoon, sir. I'm very pleased to meet you both.'

31

'Now she's here at last, I'd better ring Khartoum.' Sir Neville finished his coffee, stood up, and flashed Poppy a cunning smile that made her shiver inside. 'I'll be seeing a lot more of you in your time with us, Miss Cavendish,' he purred.

As Poppy wondered why her arrival should precipitate an international telephone call, Sir Neville left them.

His wife seemed placated by Poppy's naturally respectful disposition and her demeanour resumed its more benign expression as she showed her to her quarters, a tastefully furnished little ground floor apartment, completely self-contained, the French windows of which looked out onto a neat little patio. Then watching Poppy clasp her hands joyfully over her mouth to suppress the squeal of happiness she felt at realising how lucky she was to have landed such a perfect position, Lady Bradburn compounded her elation by quoting a starting remuneration package that seemed indecently generous to the inexperienced girl.

'Well?' she demanded. 'Will the post suit you?'

'Oh, I should say so!' Poppy gushed gratefully. 'Thank you, ma'am!'

'I'll be frank with you, Cavendish.' Lady Bradburn's eyes flitted momentarily to Poppy's breasts, but quickly rose back to her face without a hint of a clue of her inner thoughts. 'The post involves some duties of a... *sensitive* nature. Yes, that's the best way to describe them. So before I can finally confirm your appointment I must be completely assured of your total obedience and discretion at all times.'

'I always do as I'm told, ma'am, and I know how to be discreet,' Poppy guaranteed the woman, desperate to gain the confirmation for the wonderful job appointment that was tantalisingly close, thrilled by the prospect of living and working in such lovely surroundings, whilst earning what seemed to her to be such a generous salary.

'Good... good...' the woman mused. 'We have an induction system which measures whether a candidate's acceptance of our ways and methods is likely to be total. We cannot afford the slightest hint of rebellion here.' Lady Bradburn allowed her eyes to rove speculatively over Poppy's curvaceous form, seemingly assessing her closely, physically as well as mentally. 'We need to set tests, gauge responses, that kind of thing. Do you agree to this?'

'Yes, ma'am, I suppose so,' Poppy said, joining her hands meekly in front of her. 'If that's what you require then it's okay by me.'

'Good,' Lady Bradburn said again, clearly pleased by the response.

'First then,' she went on briskly, 'we must examine you. We don't believe in dilly-dallying or shilly-shallying here, so we will proceed immediately. You may take a moment to freshen up first, and I'll meet you in the hall in ten minutes. I do not expect to be kept waiting.'

'Yes ma'am, thank you, ma'am,' Poppy responded instinctively.

The lascivious events in the car with the lecherous Captain Smythe had in truth left her knickers noticeably and shamefully damp, and she was glad of the chance to wash and change.

Having hastily done so, determined to obey Lady Bradburn in every particular, she returned to the entrance hall a minute or so earlier than the designated time. Lady Bradburn appeared, on time just about to the second, and as they were about to ascend the main staircase they met a young man coming down. He was well dressed and good-looking, and there was an indefinable *something* about him that took the girl's breath away. For one thing, he simply reeked of money; from the raincoat flung carelessly over his shoulder in case needed to protect against the inconsistent summer weather, to his handmade Oxford shoes, everything about him was top of the range.

He looked at Poppy briefly, the same kind of scrutinising glance of appraisal that he might have given to an expensive sports car or piece of valuable horseflesh, and she saw with a thrill that he was totally self-assured and focussed, used to giving orders and being obeyed - accustomed to power.

And in her turn Poppy experienced a strong feeling of the complete opposite, her only wish to please and appease, to serve in whatever way would best satisfy him, to subjugate herself to his masculine command - above all to obey.

'Ah, Robert,' Lady Bradburn said. 'This is Poppy Cavendish, whom I'm about to interview for the post as our new personal assistant.' She turned to the mesmerised girl, still gawping at the young man, and said with obvious pride, 'Cavendish, this is my son, Robert.'

'You do get all the fun, mother,' Robert chuckled knowingly, and Poppy thought she might swoon there and then as he flashed her a smile of perfect white teeth, jauntily carried on past them down the remaining steps and headed across the hall for the front door.

Reluctantly tearing her gaze from him as he disappeared outside and the front door closed behind him, Poppy followed Lady Bradburn upstairs and along the landing. They turned left and then right, ascended a smaller flight of stairs, and went through a maze of narrow corridors to a door rather strangely marked, in Poppy's opinion, *Induction Room.*

'Wait here.' Lady Bradburn opened it and went in without looking back, and Poppy stood in the gloomy passage for what seemed quite a long time, and just when she was beginning to wonder if she would ever by summoned, Lady Bradburn called, 'You may enter now, Cavendish!'

The room beyond the door was small, with something of the atmosphere of a doctor's surgery about it. And Lady Bradburn only helped to compound this atmosphere, for she was now dressed in a white coat, sitting at a desk beside a second closed door.

'Go behind the screen and take all your clothes off, including your underwear,' she ordered. 'Before we risk committing to you, you must undergo a complete appraisal, both physical and mental.'

'Yes, ma'am.' Despite trying to appear bubbly and not at all unnerved by this strange turn of events, Poppy unsurprisingly felt terribly apprehensive as she stood behind the small screen indicated and began to undress. Whatever was going to happen to her now? Was this normal procedure when trying to gain a position of employment?

When completely naked she stepped tentatively out from behind the screen into the room. 'Hmmm...' Lady Bradburn perused her mouth-watering naked form. 'Very good,' she said, then indicated the straight-backed chair in front of the desk. 'Sit here so I can put the straps on you.'

'The... the straps?' Poppy stammered as she sat down, her nakedness making her feel horribly vulnerable and adding to her growing concerns.

'I do hope you are not going to be the type who questions everything I tell you, young lady,' the woman said, taking a number of buckled leather straps from a drawer in the desk. 'If so, we'd better terminate this arrangement right now, so you'll have at least some time to make your way back to Maidenhall before dark. I do so dislike the ones who constantly prattle and question my every word. I simply won't tolerate it, do you hear?'

'Oh yes, ma'am!' Poppy insisted, even her concerns about the woman's strange procedures outweighed by the prospect of returning to Maidenhall, where lurked a stern chairman of the governors who would be extremely displeased that she'd let him and the good name of the college down. 'I'm very sorry, ma'am, I?'

'Good, that's better.' As Lady Bradburn fastened the leather straps around Poppy's wrists and ankles, the girl managed to hide her pussy by keeping her legs modestly closed, and as she was looking at the grey-haired woman she did not notice the steel rings protruding from the straps until their buckles had been pulled worryingly tight.

Lady Bradburn then pulled her hands behind her back, and Poppy heard the click of metal on metal as her wrists were clipped together. And as she tentatively tested pulling them apart, predictably without success, Lady Bradburn was doing the same thing to her ankles, moving her feet together so she could snap the straps to each other.

The woman then straightened up and stood close to Poppy, the hem of the white coat touching the bound girl's naked knees.

'Before coming here you did understand that I would have to examine you thoroughly, Cavendish, as a matter of procedure?' Lady Bradburn said, casually reaching out to stroke Poppy's cheek, and then brush her fringe lightly off her forehead in a manner the girl could easily have interpreted as affectionate if she didn't think that too silly to even consider. 'Thoroughly and *intimately*,' the woman added mysteriously.

'N-no, ma'am,' Poppy mumbled, remembering Miss Sharpe's unsettling warning about saying too much, and not wanting to incur the wrath of Lady Bradburn, who had made it very clear how she felt about petty recusants, 'I - I didn't know that, but?'

'You may have a minute to prepare yourself,' the lady said, with what she probably considered to be compassion. 'When you are ready, follow me into the next room. If you do so, I will know then that you have accepted our conditions. If you do not, then you will be returned to Maidenhall forthwith. The choice is yours...'

She went through the second door, and before it closed Poppy caught a glimpse of the room beyond, and it made her shiver with dread. Whatever were

34

those strange metal structures she spied? She felt terribly isolated and bemused by the bizarre way things were developing, but what could she do except follow?

So she took a deep breath, stood up and began to move, but because her feet were bound so closely she found she could only shuffle with infinite slowness. Her stuttering motion and the way her hands were fastened behind her back made her breasts quiver firmly, but she managed to enter the second mysterious room.

What Poppy saw there made her blood run cold. To her left, a heavy steel chain hung from a hook in the ceiling, a series of buckled leather straps attached to its end. To her right there stood a metal cage, about five feet high, with a triangular steel seat in one corner, manacles suspended from its roof and leg-irons bolted to its floor.

For a moment she wondered where the woman had gone, but then she spoke from over her shoulder, making her jump and turn in alarm.

'On this first occasion you may choose your method of restraint, Cavendish,' she said.

To compound Poppy's agitation, Sir Neville was there too, also wearing a white medical coat, and as they both moved purposefully towards Poppy she looked fearfully at the solid wooden chair sitting portentously on its own in the centre of the room. Its stout square arms and legs were fixed to a heavy base, and she eyed with trepidation the steel rings bolted strategically to it.

'She seems to have an eye for the chair,' Sir Neville suggested, and his wife nodded approvingly as they led Poppy to the menacing piece of furniture. 'The girl has taste. A wise choice indeed.'

Sir Neville's eyes roved over Poppy's naked body. 'What an interesting vision you present, young lady,' he droned salaciously. 'I do hope you understand the full merits of unwavering discipline?'

'I'm sorry, sir?' Poppy said, not quite sure what he was on about.

'You will be,' he mused cryptically, and as his wife bent to adjust something under the wooden chair, Poppy was shocked to feel his finger worming its way between the tight cleft of her buttocks, where it quivered lewdly against her anal rim. 'You may sit down now,' he told her.

The seat of the chair was cold against Poppy's bare bottom, and she was both disconcerted yet strangely excited when Sir Neville went behind her and wrapped a strap around her neck like a collar, which he clipped to a ring on the chair's high back.

Lady Bradburn attached her ankle straps to rings on the front legs close to the floor, and fixed her arms behind her in a way that made her breasts jut vulnerably and enticingly.

Modesty made Poppy keep her thighs tightly together while all these bizarre preparations were going on, but Sir Neville next looped a strap around her right knee and his wife did the same with her left. They pulled these through a ring at the back of the chair, moving and keeping her legs wide apart, and she heard the straps being clipped together.

Having completed the task of securing the girl, the couple stood back and regarded her with evident satisfaction and relish. Up until that moment they had acted as though what they were doing was a completely normal aspect of the job candidate selection process. But now, without any warning, their demeanours changed completely and worryingly.

'You are in our power now,' Sir Neville announced dramatically, fastening greedy hands on her breasts, which he cupped and squeezed in a most unrestrained manner. As Poppy squirmed in a fruitless effort to escape his cold touch, which made her nipples stiffen even as panic gripped her being, Lady Bradburn slid a hand down to her pussy, parted her sex lips and touched her clitoris.

'We can do anything we like with you,' she said. 'And believe me, we are going to do just that!'

Sir Neville bent to kiss Poppy wetly, and forced his tongue inside her mouth. To Poppy the fervent kiss seemed to go on for a long time, and when he eventually broke away she was shocked to be confronted with the distortion of his white medical coat, something within at around waist height tenting it obscenely towards her flushed face.

'Better see what we've got here, that we've not been short-changed,' he said, and nodding her agreement, his wife wheeled over a small trolley with a lamp and a round mirror attached to it. She directed it between Poppy's legs and switched the lamp on, bathing the bound girl's sex with a circle of light, illuminating it for them to inspect all the easier. With the air of a surgeon about to perform a major operation the lady then adjusted the mirror until she had it just right for her purposes.

'We take it you are still a virgin, Cavendish?' Sir Neville asked.

'I, um, y-yes, sir,' Poppy stumbled, taken aback by the directness of such a personal question.

'Hmmm...' he pondered. 'Let's hope so, eh? That is one definite proviso as to whether we accept you or not. As Smythe well knows.'

As Poppy wondered why the condition of her hymen should be of any consequence to them, Lady Bradburn snapped on an almost translucent pair of white rubber surgical gloves, stooped and began to examine Poppy's sex, paying particular attention to her labia and then the bud of her clitoris. She then parted the moistened lips, straightened a finger, and Poppy held her breath and watched wide-eyed as the digit slid slowly and inquisitively inside her.

'We'll have no problems with this one, Neville,' the severe woman eventually decided, extracting her glistening finger and stripping off the rubber gloves, before dropping them into a metal dish on the trolley. 'She's telling the truth. She's definitely still intact.'

'Excellent,' enthused her husband, and then, showing less discretion than his wife, he placed his own finger against Poppy's pussy and pushed it into her with no time for incidentals like rubber gloves, the bound girl unable to suppress a gasp of discomfort and pleasure as it wormed its way into her tight opening.

'Careful, dearest,' Lady Bradburn admonished, 'or she'll be worthless.' She put an arm around the girl's slender shoulders and said, 'I'm pleased to pronounce you *virgo intacto*.' And then her mouth tightened. 'Now for your *real* test, and a chance for you to display true obedience.'

'The way you behave now will decide finally whether we employ you,' Sir Neville said, 'or whether we send you onto the streets of Burchester.'

Poppy could not imagine losing such a perfect position of employment before she'd even begun, so she determined that no matter what form the 'test' took, she would comply without protest.

The intense couple unclipped the steel rings on her collar, her wrists and ankles, stood her up and turned her around to face the chair. Sir Neville re-clipped her wrist and ankle straps to steel rings, turned her slave collar until its ring was at the front, and attached it to the top of the chair's high back.

Then leaving Poppy pinioned at their mercy with her bottom thrust out, Lady Bradburn went to a cupboard. The wide-eyed girl strained to turn her head, and as she caught the impression of fearsome implements hanging in rows inside the cupboard she felt Sir Neville's finger working its way between her buttocks again. As it circled her anus she wondered if his wife knew he was taking every opportunity to fondle her. Lady Bradburn then returned with something Poppy could not see, which she handed to her husband.

'I'm going to use this to test your obedience,' Sir Neville announced, and held an ornate rattan carpet beater before Poppy's fearful eyes. Despite her bizarre predicament she could not but help thinking how absurdly out of place it looked in the sterile confines of the small room. 'When I strike it across your buttocks you must not flinch, rather you should try to move towards it,' she just heard him say through her spinning thoughts.

Poppy waited, her face a mask of trepidation, and then her hips jerked away involuntarily as the carpet beater passed by harmlessly, so close that she felt a rush of air on her cheeks.

'My, you are a disobedient one, aren't you?' Sir Neville murmured reprovingly. 'If you obey me, however, my wife will reward you.' A feminine hand stole between Poppy's legs, located her clitoris with precision, and agitated it in a manner that quickly had the girl moaning with pleasure. Then almost as soon as it had started the seriously agreeable caressing stopped, and Sir Neville spoke sternly again. 'Defy us, however, and your punishment will be severe, rest assured of that!'

He raised the carpet beater above shoulder height and this time Poppy strained her shapely bottom backwards, eager to appease and please the couple.

Whack!

He brought it down with merciless strength, and she cried at the force of the blow.

'Oooowww!' she moaned. 'Oh sir, it hurts so much!'

'Be a brave girl!' Lady Bradburn encouraged, seizing Poppy's nipples and rolling them, making her enjoyment of the situation surge, and then the woman slipped a hand between the girl's trembling legs and circled her clitoris again. As intense pleasure took the girl closer to a wonderful orgasm more fingers, which she knew belonged to Sir Neville, parted her scalded, beaten buttocks, located the tiny entrance that hid there and caressed it with a circular motion that echoed the artful touch between her sex lips.

'Keep absolutely still now,' he warned. 'My wife has to photograph you for the purposes of the test.'

Lady Bradburn used a digital camera to take a close-up of Poppy's stinging bottom while Sir Neville renewed his stance. 'Maintain your position exactly,' he said, 'and this will be the last time I strike you with this particular implement. Move, and we say goodbye here and now.'

If Poppy's buttocks were still hurting from the first blow, her pussy was savouring the completely opposite sensation caused by the gentle caress that had followed. But with a supreme effort of will she pushed her bottom back again as far as her restraints allowed, and felt Sir Neville smoothing his palm over the raised pattern of pain.

Whoosh!

This time when the beater passed in a rush of air she felt a delicious tingle in her clitoris, and let out a cry of mixed desire and relief. A moment later the cane implement was raised again, and this time it swatted down against her buttocks with a terrific force, landing almost exactly on the first.

Thwack!

'Ooooooh, sir!' the girl cried with tears meandering down her face. 'Oh, sir... sir... sir!'

The camera flashed again.

'You have shown exemplary control,' Sir Neville praised, fractionally out of breath from the brief but forceful exertion, 'and passed your test with flying colours. Well done, my dear.'

'Th-thank you, sir,' Poppy stuttered with quiet pride.

Sir Neville took the digital camera from his wife, and when she had released Poppy and gently helped her sit on the chair, her lovely tear-streaked face wincing as her bottom made contact with the cool wooden seat, he took several portrait shots of her. His wife then gave Poppy a board to hold with the mysterious legend BH35 printed on it in large black letters, and Poppy obediently held this over her breasts while he took more photographs.

When they'd finished he asked with apparent congeniality, 'Is there anything you'd like to ask us, my dear?'

Poppy's head was still in a bit of a spin with all that had happened to her in such a short space of time, and she was finding it difficult to formulate much coherent thought. 'Um, well, I'm not really sure?'

'Good,' Lady Bradburn interrupted her. 'Now then, your main task whilst with us,' she continued, 'will be to take over certain conjugal duties of which the years have made me weary. Have you any idea what I am talking about?'

'No, ma'am, I'm not sure that I have,' Poppy admitted.

'Then let me explain a little more clearly,' Sir Neville said solemnly. 'The curriculum at Maidenhall lacks one subject, and that is sex education. So we will demonstrate your duties to you now.'

The hedonistic couple led her across the compact room to a small leather sofa, where they sat on each side of her. Then shrugging out of her white coat, Lady Bradburn, now wearing only a pair of black stockings and suspenders but looking remarkably good for her age, leaned across Poppy's naked form to kiss Sir Neville, and as the girl watched their tongues lewdly entwine her excitement at what was clearly about to happen intensified. As the aristocratic woman's hand disappeared into her husband's white coat, where Poppy could tell it was engaged in an intimate caress, Sir Neville began feeling Poppy's breasts, and soon all three were moaning and panting as their pleasure mounted.

'The first way in which you will serve my husband is by caressing his organ by hand,' Lady Bradburn said, breaking away breathlessly and giving Poppy a scandalous look. 'And since you've never yet seen a penis, let alone an erect penis, you had better prepare yourself.'

'Yes, ma'am...' Poppy whispered, thankful that they appeared to be unaware of her shameful encounter with Captain Smythe, when she'd not only seen an erect penis but sucked one until it ejaculated in her mouth and she'd swallowed everything he had to offer! But even after that experience she could not suppress a sharp intake of breath as Sir Neville's penis was exposed, and without thinking she gasped, 'Oh, sir... it's so *big*...'

She had imagined that men would generally be the same size and shape, but compared to Captain Smythe's, Sir Neville's was as thick as a truncheon, with a head as big as a peach. His wife's hand moved reverently over it.

'Perhaps you'd like to try, my dear?' she said, once she had demonstrated the movement sufficiently.

Poppy obeyed, and reached curiously to feel Sir Neville's hairy balls, secretly thrilled to feel Lady Bradburn's hand again squeeze between her thighs to seek out her swollen clitoris. Sir Neville dropped one hand to finger his wife's pussy, and for the next few minutes the room was silent save for heavy breathing as each of them made another's pleasure rise towards an inevitable crescendo. There was no doubt that Lady Bradburn was the conductor of the group, for when it seemed that Poppy might climax before her she ceased her ministrations and looked her in the eye.

'Another activity my husband enjoys immensely is oral sex,' she told the spellbound girl, then lowered her lips to Sir Neville's standing cock and let her tongue flicker across its weeping eye with a rapid side-to-side movement that made his hips arch with pleasure. She then opened her mouth wide and closed it around her husband's huge helmet. She sucked audibly and pumped her fist up and down the gnarled column until his grunts signalled that his excitement was about to peak, when she pulled away with perfect timing and looked dreamily at Poppy. 'Your turn, my dear,' she said huskily. 'But take it easy; we don't want him climaxing too soon, and I can tell that the thought of fucking your sweet mouth is nearly tipping him over the edge before you've even begun on him.

Poppy hesitated for a moment, the woman's crude language increasing her confusion, but then she lowered her head until her lips were close to the leaking eye at the very summit of Sir Neville's cock-head, when she felt a return of the trepidation she had felt with Captain Smythe that morning. She opened her mouth to request a reprieve, but as she did so the scheming woman's hand moved to the back of her head and pressed. As the bulbous tip of Sir Neville's cock eased her lips further apart and filled her mouth, pressed to the back of her throat, she felt the same inexplicably delicious sensation of submission and surrender the captain's dominance had unearthed earlier. Knowing she had gone well beyond any point of no return, Poppy sucked avidly, getting accustomed to the feel of a powerful cock stretching her mouth open until Sir Neville's responses became increasingly animated and his wife drew a halt to them going any further.

She pulled Poppy's hand between her own thighs, and as the girl's inexperienced fingers worked on her she began to pant, closing her eyes and feeling her own breasts. When her climax was almost upon her she pulled away, climbed up onto the sofa on her knees, straddled Poppy's thighs and smothered the awestruck girl's face with her soft, scented breasts and cleavage.

'But the prime mode of sexual activity,' she whispered sensuously, 'and the only one you will *not* be allowed to perform with my husband, is fucking. Show her, Neville.'

The autocratic gentleman stood up behind his wife, and Poppy watched with fascination through the woman's parted thighs as his fat cock slowly disappeared into her until only his dangling balls were visible. Instinctively the girl reached out to cup their swaying weight in her palm, which seemed to please the couple, and as she did so Lady Bradburn eased her down onto her back, shuffled forward with her husband still snugly docked, and squatted over Poppy's glowing face.

'Lick, my dear,' she instructed. 'Lick.'

Poppy found the clitoris and worked it until her tongue ached, and as Sir Neville pumped his stout pillar of flesh in and out of his wife's squelching pussy she could feel his hairy testicles slapping her chin and the thick vein on the underside ploughing against her tongue-tip with every thrust.

Lady Bradburn pressed down harder onto Poppy's face, and realising that the couple were intent only on their own pleasure and not interested in hers, the supine girl slipped one hand down her body and started to finger herself. She continued to caress Sir Neville's swinging scrotum with the other hand, and he responded by grunting more and more urgently. As his excitement approached its peak he introduced a circular motion to his rhythm, and Poppy heard Lady Bradburn braying with passion as her orgasm also approached.

They pressed down harder, covering Poppy's face with the woman's carnal juices, and to heighten his paroxysm of ecstasy Sir Neville croaked, 'In your mouth, girl!' and pushed his scrotum over Poppy's face, displacing his wife's clitoris from her tongue. 'I want you to suck my balls into your mouth!'

Frigging herself urgently as her orgasm crept closer, Poppy would have been glad to accede to his order, but his wife had other ideas. Aware that her husband was about to ejaculate, she reached down to grip his cock and pulled it briefly out of her cunt so that his first extended eruption of semen shot partly into

Poppy's open mouth, but mostly over her startled face. A moment later the woman, greedy for his spunk, fed her husband's palpitating cock back into her sex and was groaning deeply as she rubbed her clitoris over Poppy's sperm-covered face. As the couple's climax took hold they pushed down harder and harder, smothering the girl's face with genital flesh, and only when the woman had wrung every last vestige of pleasure from the passionate coupling did she pull away. Sir Neville withdrew his slowly wilting cock, and more semen dripped from the hovering pussy and covered Poppy's flushed features.

'Well, Cavendish,' Lady Bradburn sighed as she handed her a towel, 'I rather think you've got the job. Anything you'd like to ask?'

'No, ma'am,' Poppy panted, feeling utterly exhausted, the enormity of recent events catching up with and overwhelming her.

The overbearing couple led Poppy back through the maze of corridors and down staircases. She was still naked, and when they left her in the cosy apartment she was disconcerted to hear a key turning in the lock. Why had they done that? What was the purpose of confining her to the apartment? As much as she loved it and the privacy it offered her - privacy such as she'd never enjoyed in her life before - the thought of being locked in was a worrying one.

At a loss for what to do, and still feeling shamefully turned on, having not enjoyed an orgasm like her new employers had, she put her concerns to the back of her mind and took a shower, and the sight of her naked body in the mirror, her bottom with its ornate pattern of pain in angry red, made her feel even more randy. Her buttocks throbbed from the beating, so that when she found an electric fan in her bedroom she pointed it at the bed and turned it on. She then lay facedown with her legs open, letting the cool air waft over her whipped bottom, and after a short time she fell into a much needed doze.

In her restless dream she was fleeing from an odious blind man who wanted to fuck her with his monstrously large penis, and she could hear the regular tapping sound of his white stick on the pavement as he relentlessly pursued her.

Eventually the insistent tapping woke her, and she realised it was coming from the French windows. She thought at first it was the wind blowing a branch against the glass, but when she slipped on her dressing gown and went to investigate she was shocked to see there was a man standing outside. He was facing away from her with the collar of his raincoat pulled up, and for a moment his general bearing made her think it was Captain Smythe. Then as she wondered what to do Robert Bradburn turned and gave her a smile, so she thought it only polite to let the son of her employers in. She tried the handle and found that door was locked too, but when she looked up again Robert had already extracted a key from his coat pocket and was letting himself in.

She stepped back a pace and her heart was pounding in her chest as he casually stepped into the apartment and closed the French windows behind him. She already suspected that beyond the excitement of the newly discovered sex there lay something even greater, a something where she could be loved and valued and protected. And alone for the first time with an eligible young man, she wondered if romance could possibly blossom between them.

'H-hello, Robert,' she said, suddenly feeling clumsy in his presence, unsure of how to address him correctly.

'Robert?' he sneered, and she felt his power immediately in the arrogance with which he threw his raincoat onto the back of one of the two armchairs in the cosy apartment, into which he sprawled. His head went back, he gave a contemptuous snort of laughter, and she glimpsed his perfect white teeth as he demanded, 'Do you dare call my father by his first name?'

'N-no.' Poppy blushed crimson and experienced an unwanted and unexpected flutter in her pussy. 'I mean no, Mr Bradburn.'

Robert looked at her like something he might have trodden on in the park, then in a confident tone he ordered her to call him 'sir', just as she had to his father.

'I'm sorry.' Poppy stared at her feet, feeling intimidated by his imperious confidence.

'You're sorry, *what?*' A hint of smugness in his expression betrayed how much he was enjoying her discomfort, and made her wonder if he disliked her for some reason.

'Sir,' Poppy gabbled hastily. 'I'm sorry, sir. Her aspect was one of abject subservience, and from that moment on their relationship was cast.

'Stand beside the chair until I decide what I want to do with you.' Robert kicked off his shoes and looked at her with appraising eyes. Poppy felt a deliciously guilty thrill as she wondered what intentions he had for her. She thought of Sir Neville's erection being thrust into Lady Bradburn's wet pussy, and her excitement became tinged with unease. What if the son's penis was enormous too?

'Don't you like to look pretty?' he suddenly asked.

'I - I do, yes sir.'

'So why are you wearing that plain old thing, then?'

Poppy pulled her dressing gown tighter around herself. 'I don't know, sir.' Maidenhall had given it to her when she was fourteen. Its familiarity made it feel safe and comfortable, but she realised now that it looked desperately dowdy. 'It's all I have, I suppose,' she said candidly.

'Take it off,' he said. 'Shabbiness depresses me.'

Blushing madly with embarrassment, but desperate not to make an enemy of the man, she untied the belt and let the dreary garment fall to the floor. His eyes roved over her naked body, lingering at the softly haired delta crowning her closed and shapely thighs. She squirmed uncomfortably beneath his scrutiny, and was secretly and shockingly thrilled when he reached out and ran his hands up her smooth flanks to her breasts. He stroked their fleshy perfection for some time, and then squeezed them so sharply she squealed in mixed excitement and pain and shock.

'Turn sideways,' he commanded, and she obeyed feeling strange to be naked while he was fully dressed. She stood meekly as he placed a palm flat against her glossy pubic curls, while his other coasted tenderly over the red imprints of anguish created by his father.

'I see you've already been punished,' he mused. 'How dare you present yourself to me as damaged goods?'

'But, sir,' Poppy protested, 'it wasn't my fault, I?'

'You're going to blame my parents, are you?' he demanded, his chin thrust forward aggressively.

'N-no, sir.' Poppy swallowed her pride, and humbly added, 'I'm very sorry, sir.'

'And so you should be. Now stand there,' he pointed at the carpet between his languidly spaced feet, 'facing me, between my legs.' When Poppy had obeyed he went on. 'Bend forward from the waist, keeping your legs and torso straight.' She adopted the posture he demanded, and it became immediately obvious that her breasts were to be the focus of his attention, for he cupped and stroked them possessively. 'Do you know that your tits present a wickedly licentious aspect to me, Cavendish?' he drawled.

'Ah, well no, sir,' she said falteringly.

'Well they do, oh yes, and I propose to punish them for it,' and with no further warning he administered a series of sharp, pitiless slaps to first the outside of one breast and then the other, and when they began to glow a painful red he cruelly squeezed her nipples.

'Now straighten up and move closer,' he said, and an impatient nudge with his hand against the inside of her thighs made Poppy partially open her legs, and her obedience was recognised when his fingers moved up between them. With a lightness and sensitivity of touch surprising in one whose attitude was one of such uncompromising self-importance, they traced the outline of her pussy several times before venturing against the rapidly moistening valley at its core. If the succulent flesh of Poppy's inner lips had not given away the whereabouts of her clitoris, the little organ itself would soon have done so for it was already evidently stiff, as though begging to be found.

Robert rested his free hand on the girl's punished buttocks while his other squeezed her dampening inner lips in a way that was surprisingly gentle, and when the tip of his middle finger coasted lightly over her sensitive clitoris, Poppy's hips began to move forward and back with gathering passion. She panted audibly, longing to turn her nipples in her fingers now that his punishment of them had made them hungry for more attention, an impulse she resisted because she was not sure how he would react. If things carried on like that, she thought in mounting confusion, she was going to utterly embarrass herself and orgasm there and then! And although still relatively unversed in the ways of the flesh, Poppy had already learned enough to realise that the antidote needed to quell her passions was a hefty dose of pain.

'S-sir,' she ventured desperately, sliding her pussy to and fro over his fingers, 'you... you can spank me... if you think I deserve it, and if you'd like to.'

'Oh, may I?' he jeered sarcastically. 'I need an invitation to spank a member of the staff now, do I?' Despite his derision he withdrew the hand that was causing her such reprehensible delight, and without warning slashed the flat of its palm down in a contemptuous swipe across the ridges of pain caused by her earlier beating. Then he sprawled back and withdrew a small flask of whisky from a pocket of the raincoat draped over the back of the chair, from which he tipped back his head and drew a long swig. The excitement in her tummy turned to pain in her buttocks, and she glanced nervously down at the front of his expensive trousers and saw them lifted by an inner swelling, looking as rigid as a bone.

'I'll even flog you when the fancy takes me,' he said sneeringly, 'but that won't be until your skin is clear.' He flipped the top of the flask back on and set it on the occasional table beside the chair. 'And now I think it's time we had ourselves a little more fun,' he ruminated.

Poppy wondered how Sir Neville and Lady Bradburn would react if they knew or found out what was going on between her and their son. Would they be angry, perhaps dismissing her before she'd even started in her new position? Or were they so liberally perverse that they'd condone or even encourage it? With these bewildering thoughts racing around her poor head, Poppy suddenly realised that Robert Bradburn, still lounging in the armchair, had opened and pushed his trousers to his knees, exposing his silk underwear to her reluctantly captivated gaze.

And he was actually brazenly playing with himself through the sheer material, an inflexible protuberance pointing upwards as it strained to be free, and she drew in a sharp breath of covert excitement as she realised he was already fully erect.

'Touch it,' he coaxed, moving his hand away and indicating the silk-covered column, which pulsed slightly but visibly as Poppy gazed down at it rising from his lap. 'I want you to play with me through my underwear until I tell you otherwise.'

Tentatively, Poppy reached down and traced the shape of his penis and balls with her fingers, then enclosed the silk-encased stake of living flesh in her fist, merely holding it for a while until she gathered some confidence, and then moving it up and down, unsure at first but gaining in belief as she detected a dreamy enjoyment of her cautious ministrations in his expression.

Very slowly Robert started to move his hips in time with her movements, and when he put one hand to the back of her head, pulled her closer and kissed her passionately, Poppy was amazed but entranced. Then he mumbled an instruction for her to pull the waistband of his underwear down, and as she mutely obeyed his vibrant cock sprung and swayed powerfully into view.

Poppy was unsure just how she felt, seeing such a mesmerising example of manhood. Was she in awe of it or fearful of it? At that moment she was too confused by her tumbling emotions to know.

'Kneel down,' he ordered, breaking the spellbinding silence between them. 'Between my thighs,' and as Poppy obeyed dutifully, kneeling tight against him as though worshipping at an altar, she stared at the leaking little eye of his penis as he took her chin in his hand, tilting her face up to his. 'You know what I want from you now, don't you?'

For one so relatively inexperienced Poppy did know, only too well, and said clearly, 'Yes sir, I do.' She lowered her head humbly and opened her mouth, as Robert reached between them, took her nipples between his fingers and thumbs and rolled them gently, permeating sensations of pleasure down to her pussy.

'What a lovely mouth you have, Poppy,' he said. 'Now I want to feel it giving my cock a good, hard, long suck.'

Poppy licked inquisitively, and found that she enjoyed tracing the column's shape with her tongue, and an instinctive knowledge of how to react made her reach between them and caress the shaft with one hand, the forefinger of the other stroking his scrotum. Soon his cock were glistening with saliva, and when Poppy gingerly took the purple helmet into her mouth and sucked Robert groaned his satisfaction and his pinching of her nipples intensified, her secret, smouldering pleasure complementing the delicious pain perfectly. Very soon his chest was heaving as her attentions pleased him immensely, his obvious pleasure betrayed by his gasps and groans.

'Stop now,' he eventually warned, and then sat with his eyes closed for a few minutes while his breathing and his arousal slowly calmed.

Poppy knew that he feared coming too soon, curtailing his enjoyment prematurely, and wondered what his plans for her were, part of her hoping and part of her dreading that he would fuck her, as she stayed on her knees and stared at his cock in wonder. Fascinated by its bonelike rigidity, she intuitively pursed her lips and touched a delicate kiss against the underside of its plum-like helmet.

'It's my turn now,' he eventually said, his voice slightly less strained than when he last spoke to her.

Due to his state of undress, Robert swapped places with the lovely girl somewhat clumsily, and on his knees, pulled her legs apart and without pausing buried his handsome face between her thighs, and it took a split second for Poppy to realise that he was doing what up until that moment she would have considered unthinkable - he was licking and sucking her most intimate place!

Poppy felt a wave of revulsion, a fascinated horror tinged with intense excitement, for Robert's tongue and lips were stirring exquisite sensations in her very core. She lay back in the chair, closed her eyes, and fingered her nipples as he parted her sex lips with his thumbs so he could lap her even more closely. Soon her hips were grinding up and down as her pleasure increased, and when she felt an orgasm approaching she thought she must faint.

'Sir...' she tried to pull away with a girlish squeal. 'Sir, it's too much for me!'

He turned his face up to hers, his chin wet and glistening with her juices, and closed one hand into a loose fist which he turned upwards with his middle finger extended stiffly. Poppy watched, transfixed with fascination and trepidation, as his tongue came out and circled his lips in a leer that was grotesquely carnal. His gaze caught hers and held it. As the motion of his tongue changed to a lascivious circular movement, he wormed his finger between the lips between her thighs and touched her clitoris. It was a fleeting caress, but it made her body pulse with sexual tension and the pleasure of such intimacy.

'Open your legs wider,' he urged, and pushed her knees apart. 'Now I'm going to fuck you properly. It's what we both want.'

'But, sir,' Poppy objected, her desire for Robert and her fear of what his parents might do if they ever found out about this illicit liaison and the loss of her virginity pulling her in different directions, 'your mother said I mustn't. If I do they'll find out and we'll both be in terrible trouble.'

'They've examined you, haven't they?' he asked rhetorically.

'Yes sir, they have,' Poppy acknowledged, discomfiture making her shudder, remembering the way the Bradburns had examined her so intimately.

'They'll never find out, then,' he stated, with so much certainty that Poppy wondered with a sense of gloom if he'd seduced many previous employees of his parents.

His finger returned to her tight entrance, penetrated it to the depth of its first joint, and started to rock in and out. 'They won't examine you again,' he persisted, 'and my father won't show any interest in fucking you... well, not in the usual sense of the word, at least,' he mused, chuckling salaciously.

Poppy had no time to ponder the meaning of his response as he forced his finger further into her, making her shudder with discomfort and desire. She flinched, trying to pull away, but the armchair offered no escape and after a time his finger was slipping in and out of her tight channel with less discomfort. And when he bent to press his face between her legs again, and his slithering tongue teased her clitoris as he finger-fucked her, Poppy was too far gone with pleasure to resist. As she began to moan and pant, rolling her head from side to side on the back of the armchair, he straightened up, gripped behind her knees and dragged her bottom forward, bringing her cunt within reach of his cock. Poppy could not help watching as he held the bloated tip of his penis against the sex lips his finger had just breached. To begin with he pushed very gently, at the same time squeezing her clit between finger and thumb in a way that took her to the brink of an orgasm.

But as his bulbous cock-head nudged its way into her, a sharp pain gripped her and drove any pleasure away.

'Oh, *sir*,' she cried, tears of frustration meandering down her cheeks, 'I can't take it... you're too big for me.' She looked down at her pussy, realised it was impaled by a living spear of manhood for the very first time, and fell at once into the most overwhelming orgasm of her life, a sexual climax in which intense, breathless pleasure was wrapped in a cloak of beautiful pain. The combination was overwhelming.

Robert began to fuck Poppy, using every forward thrust to drive his rigid penis deeper and deeper into her, but in spite of his strength and enthusiasm the tightness of her pussy made its inward progress slow.

'On the floor,' he grunted impatiently, and Poppy obeyed submissively. As she lay there with her legs parted wide he climbed onto her again. She caught a glimpse of his stiffly waving penis before he took her ankles in his hands, bent her double and pressed her toes to the floor on either side of her head. He then penetrated her again and resumed his onslaught at the same pace as before, eventually gasping, 'Oh yesss... that's good... nearly there!'

46

As Robert's excitement roared nearer he pumped with his cock mercilessly, harder and harder, sinking into her to the hilt, his groin slapping audibly against her upturned bottom, and despite the intense discomfort of her squashed and cramped position, Poppy felt her pleasure growing again in response.

'Oh, Poppy, yes!' he growled, and then he withdrew his penis and ejaculated into her pubic hair and onto the backs of her thighs. 'Yes!' he hissed triumphantly, allowing her to stretch her limps out again and slumping down onto her exhausted, supine form. 'Oh, yes... that was *good*.'

As they lay together, covered in a sheen of sweat, each could feel the gradually slowing pounding of the other's heart, until he eventually got to his feet and started straightening his clothes, raising and fastening his trousers.

'Sir...' her complexion rosy from the intensely ardent exertion, her voice had a pleading note as she said, 'won't you stay with me?'

'Won't I what?' he scoffed hurtfully. 'Don't be so silly, girl.' He went into the bathroom and she heard him urinating loudly into the toilet bowl as he called, 'What if mother finds out?' He came back into the room with his wallet already open, took out two new fifty pound notes and dismissively threw them down onto her breasts. 'You're not going to tell anyone what just happened, now are you?'

'I, well, no sir,' she pledged.

'And you'd better not,' he warned. 'You're involved in a power game far beyond your comprehension. If you want to come through it in one piece, you'll have to be a good girl. Got that?'

'Yes, sir,' Poppy said, although she had no idea what he was talking about. 'I think so, sir.'

And then he was gone, slipping back out into the night through the French windows whence he came.

Poppy sat glumly in the armchair for a time, and as she turned the pair of crisp notes over and over in her hands, tears trickled from her eyes as realised he'd treated her like a common prostitute. Did he think she was there to be used like his whore, and cast aside when he was done with her? She managed to ignore the frisson of excitement that tingled in her clitoris at a situation where passivity and sexual submission came together as one. The orgasms Robert had given her had been intense, and she felt so fulfilled and satisfied that the allure of sexual slavery was easy to dismiss.

After a while she got up and stood before the full-length mirror. Her breasts and bottom were still red from the beatings they had received. Poppy slipped a nightdress on and then her Maidenhall dressing gown again, and felt sad because it had lost the comfortable snugness of old and now seemed merely cheap. But then she cheered herself up by reflecting that now she was earning she would be able to buy a new dressing gown, indeed a whole new wardrobe.

Chapter 4

'Wake up!' Poppy opened her eyes, and found herself looking at a pair of attractive breasts encased neatly in a black dress and the white lacy bib of an apron, and thought for one moment that she was having another of her erotic dreams. 'Come on, Sleeping Beauty.'

As the Bradburns' pretty housemaid moved away and opened the heavy curtains, Poppy glanced appreciatively at the shape of her neat buttocks beneath her black maid's dress.

'You'll find your breakfast in the kitchenette,' the maid informed her. 'I'll be back soon to look after your bottom.'

The strong sunlight that streamed into the room made Poppy cover her eyes, and she listened to the maid leaving and closing the door behind her, noting disconsolately that the key was turned in the lock again.

She got up, washed and showered, slipped on her dressing gown before getting dressed, and went through to the kitchenette to poor some cold milk onto the bowl of cereal she found there and make herself a mug of coffee. As she ate, leaning against the kitchen worktop and gazing out onto the lovely garden, she wondered what the maid had meant by looking after her bottom.

Just as she finished the tasty bowl of milk and cereal the apartment door unlocked and opened again, and the returning housemaid soon answered the unasked question.

'What's your name?' Poppy asked politely.

'Jessop,' the girl told her.

'Don't you have a first name?'

'Yes of course I have, it's Lucy,' the maid replied indifferently, 'but you're not allowed to use it. Familiarity is frowned upon here.' Lucy Jessop's manner remained curt and peremptory. 'Now get your dressing gown and nightie off and go and lie facedown on the bed.'

'W-what are you talking about?' Poppy asked, flustered by the strange directive. 'Why on earth should I do that?'

'Lady Bradburn's orders.' Jessop looked at Poppy with intent and produced a tube of antiseptic cream. 'She wants your bottom looked after.'

Poppy didn't want to upset someone who might just become a friend or ally at some time in the future, so despite feeling embarrassed, she removed her dressing gown and nightdress and lay down naked on the bed as she'd been told to. Being respectfully obedient to Miss Sharpe or the Bradburns was one thing, but being so for a girl of a similar age and standing was humiliating. And to make matters even worse, when Jessop moved close the nearness of her and her naturally fresh fragrance made Poppy shiver secretly with excitement.

The wardrobe with a mirrored door faced the side of the bed, and in its reflection Poppy watched Jessop squeeze a dollop of cream onto her palm and begin spreading it into her welted bottom.

'Ouch!' Poppy winced, wondering if the unnecessarily brusque action was accidental or deliberate as one of Jessop's nails dug into a particularly tender area of her buttock. 'Be careful, can't you?' she complained.

'Sorry, I'm sure,' Jessop said scornfully, throwing back her dark hair and pouting. After that she was more careful, probably more out of concern about getting into trouble with Lady Bradburn than with any consideration for the prone girl, who actually began to enjoy the treatment once it was underway and under control. Despite Jessop's testy manner Poppy found her attractive in a physical sense, and resting her cheek on her folded arms she gazed in the mirror at the profile of her lovely breasts, hugged by the sexy dress and white apron bib, and gave way to a fantasy in which she sucked their alluring perfection.

Jessop kept her expression aloof and remote, but there were signs that she was enjoying giving the massage as much as Poppy was increasingly enjoying receiving it. At one point Poppy felt cool air touching the sensitive skin around her anus as her buttocks were eased apart, and saw the maid looking at it with a close attention that she found hard to fathom out.

'Whatever are you doing?' she asked.

'Sorry,' the girl said, reaching for the cream and replacing the cap. 'I've finished for today.' She went to the door and immediately returned with a bag of clothes that had been sitting in the hall. 'You're to wear these while you're here,' she announced. 'Sir and ma'am like the staff to have a degree of uniformity about them.

'Lady Bradburn is away for the day, and she has told me to tell you that, as this is your first full day here, you may take it off and acquaint yourself with your apartment. But she does not take kindly to her staff wandering the house, so you will remain here. There are books,' she indicated the small bookshelf in the small lounge, 'and the television, of course. You may amuse yourself however you so wish.'

A question came to mind about when Poppy would actually be expected to learn and start her new job. 'I?'

'I will look in on you from time to time, and you will find food in the kitchenette.' She moved to the apartment door and opened it, before looking back at Lady Bradburn's new and bemused personal assistant. 'To help you feel more at home with your new surroundings I am under instruction not to lock your apartment door, but I must stress; you are not to wander the house under any circumstances. If you do and you are caught you will be dealt with severely, believe me. Now relax and have a nice lazy day, you lucky thing,' and with that she was gone.

Poppy stared at the closed door for a few moments, and then decided to get dressed. From the bag and onto the bed she placed three black skirts, three pairs of white knickers, three matching lacy white bras, three crisply laundered white blouses, and a pair of neat black court shoes, her thoughts spinning furiously as she did so.

Why had she been delivered the previous day if the Bradburns were not yet ready to commence her employment? And why did they previously feel the need to lock her into the apartment like a criminal? It was actually beginning to feel as though she'd been sent to an open prison - or after the perverse activities of the previous afternoon and evening, a weird bordello of some sort - rather than a place of work as a personal assistant to a sir and a lady.

By late morning Poppy was bored. She'd started two books, but could not get into either of them. She'd watched some mind-numbing morning television, toured the small apartment more than once - which took about five minutes on each occasion - gazed out at the manicured garden, and was feeling more and more cooped-up and unsettled.

At one point she heard a snipping noise in the garden. She ambled with little interest to the French windows and looked out, seeing a young man pruning some shrubs. He was wearing baggy overalls, and had his back to her so she couldn't see his face, but he had nice long hair and broad shoulders. She wanted to tap on the locked glass door and call to him, just to strike up a conversation with someone to break the boredom, but she dithered, the threat of incurring the wrath of her employers ever-present in her mind, and just as her knuckle wavered in front of the glass he picked up the sack he'd stuffed the shrub debris into and disappeared from view. She'd had her chance of some human interaction, no matter how brief it might have been, and now it was lost.

However, seeing the gardener had sparked something deep within her - something perhaps akin to mischievous rebelliousness.

Why should she remain as a virtual prisoner? She wanted to see more of her new home and working environment, so why shouldn't she? Surely the Bradburns - bizarre though they apparently were - were not so draconian that they'd punish her for doing something so inconsequential?

Then Robert Bradburn came to mind, and she felt her spirits plummet with the realisation that he was probably a total love-rat. He'd seduced her, taken her virginity, and scurried off pretty damn quick. And his confident assurance that his parents would not find out that he'd plucked her virginity, made her wonder again if other girls or how many other girls had passed through the place before her. Was she travelling along some sort of conveyor-belt in the control of others, with no will of her own? And if other girls had preceded her, where were they now?

Shrugging away such uncharacteristically gloomy thoughts, Poppy decided to hell with it; she would explore the house - well, as much of the ground floor as she could, at least. It didn't seem right that she should go upstairs and intrude upon the privacy of their bedrooms.

Cautiously leaving the confines of her snug apartment, she first found the lounge, which was beautifully decorated and filled with antiques. Then she did a quick tour of the dining room, popped her head around the door of the study - that particular room did make her consider their privacy more than the previous two, so she did not enter - a small library, and then she found herself standing in the capacious hall wondering where to go next. She gazed up the sweeping stairs, tempted after all, but was just thinking that venturing up there unaccompanied really would be too difficult to explain away if discovered, when she noticed a narrow corridor beneath the stairs leading off the main hall she was in.

The house seemed remarkably - and somewhat disconcertingly - quiet. Where was Sir Neville, where was Robert, where was Lucy, and where was any other member of the household, staff or otherwise?

Damn it, she thought. If nobody had the courtesy to look after her as a new addition to the staff, then she could not be blamed for trying to relieve her boredom and familiarise herself with the place, so she started along the gloomy corridor.

There were some doors on either side, all of which were locked, and then, at the far end in the deepening shadows, she heard a haunting echo of a man's voice, which actually sounded like a muted cry of pain.

The sound was disturbing, and although the more cautious side of Poppy's nature told her to ignore it and head back to the safety of her apartment and spend the afternoon reading or watching television, her conflicting and natural curiosity found her tiptoeing cautiously towards it.

Finding a little staircase - narrow, dusty wooden steps - she took a deep breath and began to descend as quietly and carefully as possible. The agonised groaning was getting closer, and as she reached the bottom of the small flight of steps it grew even louder, and she realised it was not a groaning induced by suffering after all.

She was now standing in a dingy, low, spider web infested passage, and it took a massive effort of stubborn determination not to turn and flee, and she felt more alone and vulnerable than she ever remembered feeling in her life before. But although she knew it was not the sensible thing to do, she gathered her courage and moved stealthily towards the door beyond which the haunting sounds emanated.

She heard more groaning, and then jumped visibly as harsh slapping noises followed and Lucy Jessop's voice barked in admonition. She glanced up nervously and noted a dusty little fanlight above the door. Fate had ordained that an ancient and broken old wooden chair should be standing against the wall nearby, and in no time Poppy had moved it over and was standing on it, her eyes widening as she stood on tiptoe to peer anxiously through the grimy glass.

Sir Neville had his back to the door - or more accurately, his bottom to the door, for he was on all fours on an old bed. His buttocks had livid lash marks across them, but Jessop seemed to have reverted to a subservient role for she was lying on her back beneath him with his cock embedded in her mouth. Her legs were wide open, directly facing Poppy's vantage point, and one finger flickered over a glistening wet pussy. Her lips were stretched tightly around Sir Neville's great cock, and her head rocked forward and back on the thin mattress as he fucked her pretty face with increasing vigour.

The sight was too much for Poppy to bear, and she couldn't help but lift her short black skirt and slip a hand into her panties to find her pussy was already very wet. Sir Neville's excitement must have been gathering with the force of floodwater behind a dam, for his groaning resumed, and as his climax approached the supine maid wrapped one hand around the base of his balls and pulled his fleshy prong out of her mouth.

'Naughty boy!' she reprimanded, shuffling out from beneath him to stand at the side of the narrow bed. She picked up a leather slipper and hissed, 'You can't come yet, you must learn to share.'

A series of swift, sharp slaps over skin that was already red were enough to drive away Sir Neville's imminent orgasm, but did nothing to weaken his massive erection, or indeed Poppy's mounting excitement as she stimulated her clitoris in secret. He spoke gruffly, his voice thick with sexual tension, and Jessop squeezed beneath him again, this time facedown. He reached down to direct the swollen head of his penis into her little slot, and they started to fuck aggressively. Soon they began to tremble together and grunt in unison as a mutual orgasm took hold, Poppy's shapely legs almost buckling beneath her on the rickety perch as blissful sensations exploded from between her thighs and she too tumbled into an ecstatic orgasm.

Feeling utterly drained, and realising she'd been extremely foolish, for she could have easily made a noise and alerted the passionate couple to her presence, she carefully climbed down from the chair and placed it silently back where she'd found it, and crept back to the security of her apartment. She knew now why Sir Neville had not sent for her to commence her duties, and why Jessop was so indifferent towards her; the latter obviously seeing Poppy as a possible threat to her position of relative privilege within the household, apparently earned by favours of a sexual nature.

Chapter 5

Poppy had just finished a light lunch - her brow furrowed throughout as she tried to make sense of what she'd seen and experienced and what was going on in the house - and cleared away the dishes when Lucy Jessop entered the apartment. She looked angry and slightly flustered.

'Sir Neville has sent for you,' she announced tightly. 'He's waiting for you in his study.'

Despite her perverse experiences of only the day before, after what she'd witnessed before lunch Poppy felt apprehensive as she made her way to the study, her legs feeling weak and her heart beating furiously.

As she neared the closed study door she rubbed her palms against her black skirt, realising her nerves were making them damp, and she became aware that her treacherous nipples had stiffened and their outline could clearly be seen pressing against the lacy bra and crisp white blouse. But she also experienced a glimmer of a pleasant sensation in the pit of her stomach, so that she was feeling just a little more confident as she raised her hand to knock on the study door, the rude memory of the size and power of her employer's organ filling her head.

With one knuckle poised elegantly to tap on the polished oak, Poppy caught sight of herself in the large mirror hanging on the hall wall to her right. Even to her own eyes she looked good; her healthy hair sweeping her shoulders, the wholesome glow to her skin, her eye sparkling, the tailored black skirt only just reaching down to mid-thigh of her toned and shapely legs, the gentle swell of her bottom, and her breasts thrusting proudly within the white blouse.

Then remembering that it would be unwise to keep Sir Neville waiting, she gathered her wits and tapped the door with the raised and readied knuckle.

'Enter!' he called from within.

Poppy opened the barrier of the door and stepped into the study, not quite sure what to expect. The room was pleasant, panelled in oak and unmistakably masculine, the mixed odours of wood polish and pipe tobacco filling the air, a boar's head with impressive tusks glaring down from one wall, a green baize board with dozens of keys hanging close by it. Below the staring head, against the same wall, there stood a mahogany desk with polished brass fittings, and at the desk sat Sir Neville in a smart blue blazer and brown slacks.

'Take a seat, my dear,' he said, indicating the straight-backed chair beside his desk, and as Poppy perched on it, sitting with her knees primly together, her fingers intertwined on her lap, he went on.

'So, how are you settling in?' he asked, his eyes crawling deliberately up from her neat black shoes, her ankles, her knees, paused at the point where her creamy thighs disappeared into the skirt, then rose onward to the swell of her breasts. They hovered there as he absently missed her politely concise response and asked the same question again, clearly not really interested in her answer at all, and mused sagely, 'Good... good... and how are you getting on with the rest of the staff?'

'I've not seen anyone to speak to, sir, except the housemaid,' Poppy replied. 'I've been pretty well confined to my living quarters, sir. I had thought I'd start learning my job today.'

'Oh, yes.' His eyes flickered away. 'Of course.' He turned his attention to some papers on his desk, leaving her sitting there wondering why she'd been summoned, then without lifting his eyes from the documents on his desk he suddenly asked, 'Are you wearing any underwear, my dear?'

'I um, y-yes, sir,' Poppy told him, taken aback by the bluntness of the query.

'Well, let me see. Let me see.'

Despite her uncertainty Poppy felt a quiver of excitement at his demand, and gently rocked her bottom on the chair as she eased the neat skirt up her thighs to show him her white panties. He stared at the tight cotton stretched over the gentle swell disappearing between her closed thighs, a satisfied expression on his face.

'And part your legs a little,' Sir Neville ordered, dropping one hand to blatantly cup his groin through his slacks.

Poppy's mouth dropped slightly open as she watched the hand, which started to lower the zip. Shameful excitement filled her as she watched, her breasts swelling deliciously as she inhaled deeply. His hand disappeared inside his slacks, rummaged for a moment, and then withdrew, dragging with it a sturdy column of pulsing flesh.

'Oh, *sir*,' Poppy gasped, her green eyes widening as she licked her lips nervously, 'it's even bigger than I remember... but I don't think you should—'

'Hold your underwear aside,' he commanded. 'I want to play with you.'

Poppy blushed deeply with embarrassment, averted her eyes, and leaned back against the solid chair in resignation. Fresh-faced and rosy in her neat but sexy clothes, she pulled the gusset of her white panties to one side so that her pubic hair and sex lips peeped from between her thighs. One finger of his free hand then moved between her legs, impatiently tapping them further apart, and pressed with unfailing accuracy as it had done on the previous day.

'I want to see your breasts too, my dear,' he said, squeezing his clenched fist tightly around the base of his penis and drawing it up to the spherical head, producing a droplet of clear liquid that hovered and shimmered on the tip. 'Unbutton your blouse so I can see your heavenly tits.'

Poppy slowly released each button, one by one, until her blouse gaped, giving him a tantalising glimpse of her shadowy cleavage and the upper slopes of her smooth breasts nestling into the tight cups of her white bra. Then, without further orders, she pulled it from the waistband of the skirt and opened it even more for his avidly appreciative gaze. Sir Neville leaned forward and reached out with a weathered hand to cup one breast, while Poppy sat quietly with her hands resting meekly on her parted thighs, awaiting his next command.

'Stand and turn away from me, then bend and touch your toes,' he said. 'I want to check your bottom for marks.'

She obeyed obediently and bent until her hair swept down to the floor. The snug bra helped her firm breasts defy gravity, and after admiring the exquisitely toned lines of her legs for a few moments, he lifted her skirt onto the dip of her lower back and revealed her shapely bottom for his pleasure. Her buttocks were taut and round, stretched over with tight white cotton, and the gentle pouch of her sex was visible in outline, with a faint smudge of dampness running down its middle.

'Pull your knickers down,' he said, and she did with teasing slowness. 'That's enough,' he stopped her when they reached to just above her knees, and then she felt his cold fingers on her buttocks, his thumbs sinking into her perennial divide to part her cheeks slowly, like an antique collector unwrapping a long awaited and priceless acquisition. She knew what he was seeing, and was not surprised when his fingertip briefly touched the rim of her little rear aperture. A dark, furtive thrill made her simultaneously scared and excited then, for Sir Neville hooked his fingers into her knickers and lowered them further to her slightly parted ankles.

The forefinger and thumb of one hand parted her tight pussy lips, exposing succulent pink flesh for his bulging eyes. She knew he was leaning closer to her when his breath wafted through her silky pubic hairs.

'Beautiful...' he said in wonder, and for some minutes Poppy could hear the rhythmic sounds of languid masturbation behind her, a solo activity in which she was not invited to participate; merely to be the object of sensual beauty to stimulate it. After a while the sounds stopped, there was a lull when only his breathing could be heard, and then he stood up. 'You may retake your seat, dear girl,' he told her.

Poppy did so, disconcerted by but unable to tear her wide eyes from the undisguised carnality of the hefty prong of flesh that pulsed and bobbed before her face.

'Your behaviour since being welcomed into our home has been immoral and salacious in the extreme,' he suddenly accused her, taking her by complete surprise. His mood seemed to have unaccountably taken a swing for the worse, so she sat passively, not wanting to fuel the change, although his blatantly unjust charge sparked a flash of anger within her. *He* had been the one to instigate her lurid acts - him and his wife. She almost objected to his unfair statement but managed to suppress her feelings, sensing it was wise to do so.

'I'm very sorry, sir,' she whispered instead, her hands folded in her lap and her head respectfully bowed, her delicate panties still gathered around her shoes, her entire disposition one of extreme humility.

'And so you should be.' Sir Neville glared at her. 'I'm glad you recognise how shameful your lewd behaviour is and accept responsibility for it. So what do you think should be the consequences of such dubious conduct?'

Poppy wasn't sure, but she had a fair idea what he was alluding to, the corner into which he was coaxing her. 'I um... I think you should, ah, correct me, sir.' Poppy felt a blush rising in her cheeks. Nevertheless, she was conscious that an insistent pulsing from her clitoris was making her wet between the legs even as she whispered, 'I've been wicked, sir, and I believe it would do me good if you were to punish me for it.'

'Hmmm...' he pondered, 'I suspect you are very probably right. Very well, get up and bend over the desk with your skirt up around your waist.'

'Yes, sir.' Poppy obeyed and positioned herself as he'd told her to, her forearms on the desktop, exposing her peach-like, creamy buttocks for his pleasure, and peered anxiously to the side as he opened a draw, and with a sinking heart eyed the cane he lifted from its musty interior.

The knowledge that this odious implement would soon be used to beat her tender flesh made the girl shudder with foreboding, but then for some reason the sweet sound of birds singing in the garden impinged upon Poppy's thoughts. From her lowered position she could just see out through the window beside the desk, and spotted the young gardener she'd glimpsed from her apartment earlier, and longed to be out there with him, in the fresh air, free...

Poppy considered the caning she was about to receive and fear gripped her stomach, but at the same time she caught another glimpse of Sir Neville's large penis as he shuffled behind her and realised with sudden, certain clarity that these two things, the cane and the rigid spear of flesh, were the very instruments of dominance to which she somehow craved to submit. With her emotions trapped between their opposites she began to sense the true nature of her subservience, and realised that she must accept everything they chose to do to her.

She was ready.

'I'm going to warm you up a little with this cane.' His voice came from over her shoulder. She heard him positioning himself just so, the tension and the oppressive atmosphere of the study truly testing her resolve to remain bent over the desk for him to punish her...

Swat! Swat! Swat!

Three stinging blows landed across her vulnerable buttocks, one on the upper slope, one in the middle, and one on the delightful crease between bottom and thighs. There was a cruel pause, during which Sir Neville savoured Poppy's desperate sobs.

Swat! Swat! Swat!

Poppy's knuckles whitened as she bravely clenched her fists against the pain. 'Oh, sir!' she cried in distress as she strained to look back over her shoulder. His cock was still spearing from his open trousers, while his eyes devoured the red lines rising on her creamy white skin. 'It hurts so!'

'You should have thought of that before behaving so poorly, shouldn't you?' Sir Neville snapped. 'Don't let me hear you complaining about such a just punishment. Do you understand me?'

'Y-yes, sir,' Poppy sobbed quietly. 'I'm very sorry, sir.'

'Now I want you to move your feet back a little,' he told her, and again she dutifully obeyed, raising her torso and balancing on her hands instead of her forearms. 'Good, now open your legs wide... wider...'

Poppy did as he demanded, inching her feet apart, feeling utterly humbled and self-conscious. Soon she stood bent before him with her head deferentially down, her legs spread, her bottom raised and her hanging breasts being cocooned by her bra within the curtain of her gaping blouse. Sir Neville reached around her to cup and fondle them, and she knew he was pleased with the sight and feel of her because his breath wheezed a little in his excitement and his erection nudged wetly against the back of her upper thigh.

'Prepare yourself, my dear,' he panted in her ear, still mauling her breasts through her lacy bra. 'You are about to receive a thrashing you will not forget in a hurry. The previous strikes were merely a prelude to the main event.'

He straightened up and cut an experimental swipe with the cane, and Poppy knew her buttocks clenched and unclenched as the air moved behind her.

'Now, keep perfectly still, young lady...'

The cane cut the air again with a hiss and wrapped its tip agonisingly around her hip. Poppy yelped and desperately wanted to clutch her poor buttocks, but managed to repel the powerful instinct to take her weight on one hand and reach back with the other, stoically maintaining both hands flat on the desktop instead.

'Keep absolutely still now,' he warned, detecting her slight movement and desire to comfort her scalding bottom.

He brought the cane down again with considerable strength, and once again Poppy wailed as it bit almost at the same line as the previous one, leaving a band of searing pain in its wake.

Sir Neville raised the cruel cane again, and as Poppy wearily lifted her head to cast an imploring glance over her shoulder it swept down, and her wide-eyed expression froze as she waited that split second between the vicious impact and the swelling resurgence of hurt.

Sir Neville placed the cane on the desktop near her hands with his characteristically neat precision. He then reached around her waist again and began to maul her breasts, his slacks agitating her burning buttocks, his penis standing snugly between the twin globes of scalded flesh. His other hand crept between her legs and toyed with her sex. It was shamefully wet as his fingers delved, almost but not quite touching her clitoris. Poppy's legs trembled as pleasure merged with the enormity of the punishment she'd just endured, but as soon as he sensed this he straightened up, took up the cane again, and raised it.

'I'm going to continue your punishment,' he told her coldly. 'And only when I tire of this shall you have the chance of pleasure.'

Poppy's stomach churned; she doubted she could take much more.

The blows started again on the backs of her knees and worked their tormenting way up, only stopping at the lower curves of her blotchy buttocks. She sobbed the whole time, but even as she plumbed the depths of pain a part of her mind worked independently and with courage, and even as she tried to escape a torment from which there could be no deliverance, she recognised her innate subservience, her need to surrender and her yearning for degradation for what they were.

In a daze she sensed the cane being put down again. Then when a finger penetrated her pussy it brushed her clitoris, and she felt a rush of intense pleasure within. Again she was disturbed and thrilled when the moistened digit left her pussy and she felt it slipping into the tightness of her anus, breaching any natural resistance and sinking deep.

'In days gone by, my dear,' he said huskily, extracting the rude finger, 'Victorian days, for example, there was no birth control, and so to avoid the rigours of multiple or accidental childbirth couples used to indulge in a form of penetrative sex that carried no risk of pregnancy.' He paused, letting his point sink in, his breathing harsh against her ear, his bloated cock-head nudging against her readied anus, lubricated with her own traitorous juices. 'Have you any idea what I'm driving at, my dear?'

'I... I'm not sure, sir,' she said, uneasy with what she *knew* he was driving at.

Fumbling between her legs again he resumed the fingering of her clitoris that had already stirred her passions. 'Oh, *sir*,' she gasped, experiencing an aching discomfort as his smooth helmet squeezed its way into her tight rear channel. 'It'll never go in, sir,' she protested. 'You're too *big...*'

For a time he seemed to relent for his hips stopped pushing, but his fingers continued the magic that soon sent her spinning towards an abyss of sexual bliss. With her hands still planted on the desktop she straightened her arms and set her parted feet firmly for an explosive orgasm, her head hanging from hunched shoulders, and through dreamy, half-closed eyes she could see the inverted vision of the gnarled length of his cock, from dangling balls to just below where the head wedged just inside her clutching rear passage. The sinful bliss she felt made her cry out as she reached back with one hand to fondle his swaying scrotum, and she was swirling around the very edge of a wondrous orgasm when a possessive arm tightly encircled her waist and, clearly pleased by her instinctive action, he pulled her sharply back and his stout cock surged up fully into her bottom, his slacks and his pubic hair nestling against her welted cheeks, his weight resting on her back as he covered her like a farmyard animal, as Poppy closed her eyes and arched against the powerful invasion.

'And as my wife forbids me to fuck you in the normal sense,' he grunted heavily, stabbing his groin against her again, making sure he was fully embedded and clearly savouring the satisfaction and pleasures induced by being so, 'I cannot be blamed for following the examples set out by our inventive ancestors, now can I?'

'Ooohhhh, sir!' Poppy felt she would split as a great wedge of flesh was driven into her, yet in the same moment she knew, deep down, that Sir Neville had unlocked sexual barriers she wanted to explore to the full. '*Yes...*' As the pain took hold and then quickly and miraculously subsided into ecstasy she knew it was too late, that she was already crashing into a breathtaking orgasm. She climaxed strongly, and through spiralling emotions she became aware of his movements quickening and becoming irregular, staccato stabs of his hips, and then as he grunted aggressively she felt him erupt inside her rectum, stabbing his cock into her to the hilt, jerking her exhausted form, slumped on the desktop, against the creaking piece of antique furniture, his movements gradually easing as his spending subsided.

As both their breathing slowed to a more restful rate the telephone rang, abruptly disturbing the tranquillity that now cloaked the study. Still savouring such a glorious triumph Sir Neville seemed in no way inclined to curtail the moment prematurely, so he allowed the phone to ring as he held and rocked the girl's shapely hips and his cock pulsed sleepily, still embedded inside her cosseting bottom.

After a few more rings the answer-phone kicked in.

'*It's Hamid,*' an impatient, disembodied voice barked, and Poppy felt Sir Neville tense and withdraw from her. But in his haste he staggered and almost fell, and before he could snatch up the phone the voice went on. '*I'm calling about the new consignment, BH35. I'm going to have to postpone collection. The client isn't happy about the condition the last packages arrived in, specifically BH34 and BH33. You must ensure all goods are not tampered with, is that clear? Don't take us for fools, Bradburn. All consignments will be thoroughly examined as soon as unloaded here?*'

Sir Neville got to the phone and grabbed the receiver, while Poppy, sensing from his sudden change of mood that their illicit interlude was over, straightened up and tidied her clothing, carefully putting her panties back on, her feelings and thoughts in turmoil.

BH35?

She remembered the placard bearing that very code which Lady Bradburn made her hold to be photographed. They were talking about her!

'What?' Sir Neville growled into the telephone receiver, and Poppy flinched, wondering what was being said. 'When then...? No, that's not good enough,

Hamid, we'll have the next batch on our hands by then. Yes, another double consignment.' He glanced at Poppy, apparently confident that she had no idea what he was discussing... which, she supposed, beyond that it might involve her, she didn't really.

'No, no problems. I can't understand your client's concerns...' As the terse conversation continued Sir Neville turned towards the window and lowered his voice a little.

Poppy wondered what she should do, whether or not he had dismissed her, when she glanced at the baize board of keys hanging on the wall above the desk. Two keys hung from a hook under a label marked, *PA's Apartment*, and beside that another two keys hung beneath a label marked, *PA's Apartment - French Windows*.

Before she could stop herself, acting purely on impulse and not at all sure why she did it, Poppy reached up and slipped one of the latter keys off its hook and clutched it securely in her fist.

'Carry out any damned test you like!' Sir Neville thundered into the phone, then clamped his hand over the receiver again and turned to glare at her. 'You may go now,' he snapped, taking his foul mood out on her, before turning away again and resuming the long distance confrontation. 'The tampering happened at your end. Either that or while you had the goods in transit...!'

Out in the hall Poppy leaned back against the closed door for a while, trying to figure out what on earth was going on, the raised but muffled voice of Sir Neville continuing the argument on the other side of the oak divide.

Back in the relative security of the apartment she sat on the edge of the bed and recalled with increasing alarm the way the sinister Hamid had referred to his prospective cargo, and began to piece together a sketchy and frighteningly unbelievable plot in which she might just be caught up. The way she could already easily construe her existence in the house as a virtual prisoner, and the couple's insistence that she protect her virginity at all costs, it could all add up to only one thing, utterly implausible though it seemed: they were planning to sell her into some sort of twenty-first century slavery!

But even as the horror of her situation dawned, and as determined as she was not to allow such a thing to happen to her, she could not entirely ignore the perverse thrill she felt at the thought of becoming a mere possession, a chattel, a commodity to be passed around at a profit for the enjoyment of others.

Despite feeling ashamed and frightened of her body's traitorous reaction, she lay back on the bed, slipped a finger inside her panties and began to toy with herself, her fantasy building around another girl. For some minutes she imagined licking Karen Stringfellow's cunt, and longed to be doing just that right then. As her excitement grew she found herself back with Suky Desai, on her knees behind the bending girl with her tongue lapping first her pussy, and then, even more thrillingly, the rim of her tight bottom. Then her fantasy changed again and it was Lucy Jessop's hand that worked between her legs as she was coming, while Poppy excitedly sucked the housemaid's shapely breasts.

After a sweet orgasm she felt uneasy about the maid being embroiled in her fantasies. Did Lucy feel as her own subconscious evidently did? If she had expected an answer she was to be disappointed, for the girl was taciturn when she next appeared, bringing a pint of milk for Poppy, putting it in the fridge in the compact kitchenette.

'Are you going to treat my bottom with antiseptic cream?' Poppy asked, trying to gauge the girl's reaction to such a forward question. 'It's still sore.' She didn't elaborate on the fact that it had just suffered another onslaught from Sir Neville.

Without a word the maid snorted derisively and left, and Poppy was disconcerted to hear the key turning in the lock again. Why had she done that now, when she hadn't earlier? Was it on the orders of Sir Neville? Was it because he was worried that she'd overheard too much of his accomplice's ranting on the telephone? Poppy didn't like the plot that seemed to be unravelling around her. Something had to be done, she resolved. Something had to be done quickly before it was too late.

She opened her palm and gazed down at the key that nestled there. Then she broke into activity and flitted quickly to where her trunk had been left beside the wardrobe, found inside it a pair of her blue jeans, a white T-shirt and a pair of tennis shoes, all of which she'd not worn for quite some time, and changed into them.

Then she retrieved the money Robert Bradburn had disdainfully paid her from where she'd hidden it behind a pipe beneath the kitchenette sink, and stuffed the crinkled notes deep into her jeans pocket.

Then she went to the French windows, carefully put the key in the lock, anxious not to make even the slightest noise that might alert someone, held her breath, praying for it to be the right key, and then sighed deeply with relief as it turned smoothly and the lock disengaged with a quietly reassuring click.

Nervously she bit her lower lip and silently opened the glass door. When wide enough to allow her to exit she slipped out into the warm afternoon sunshine, looked left and then right, closed and relocked the French windows, and keeping close to the wall, slipped noiselessly into a border of tall, dense shrubbery.

With heart hammering in chest she picked her way towards what looked like the perimeter hedge, and having reached it without any mishaps, fortunately discovered a very slight gap in the manicured evergreen barrier just large enough for her svelte contours to squeeze through, and found herself amongst people on the outskirts of Burchester.

Chapter 6

Poppy felt unreal as she walked quickly along Snode Avenue towards the town centre, as though a great weight had been lifted from her shoulders. She remained alert, though, constantly glancing over her shoulder and keeping on her toes, for she knew her absence at the house could be discovered at any moment, and a search organised to find and bring her back.

People seemed to be staring at her, particularly men, probably because she was looking a little anxious, but she had also learnt enough over the past few days to realise it probably had something to do with the way her tight T-shirt moulded to the shape of her breasts and her snug jeans to her bottom.

She wandered to the town's stone bridge, paused halfway across to stare down into the waters of the River Burr, flowing and gurgling beneath her, and then reminded herself that she was a little exposed there and that the longer she was away from the house the bigger the risk of her absence being discovered, and hurried on into Bridge Street. At the post office she bought a stamp and an envelope and wrote a hasty letter to Karen Stringfellow, sending it poste restante.

On the move again she retraced her steps and saw what she wanted, an illuminated sign in a shop window: *Keys Cut Here*. Inside the middle-aged man in a grubby grey coat behind the counter seemed more interested in the shapely contents of her T-shirt than cutting a copy of the key she handed him, but a few minutes later he'd produced a shiny new replica and charged her a couple of pounds for doing so. Now if she got the chance she could return the key to the board in the study before it was found to be missing, or if she didn't get such an opportunity she would just have to hope no one noticed its disappearance or linked it to her. But at least she had hopefully increased her options for avoiding detection.

She paid and thanked him, receiving only a lurid leer in return, and walked away from the town centre back in the direction of the house, wishing she didn't have to return at all. It was only a strong sense of responsibility that she had to get to the bottom of what was going on, in case her suspicions were accurate and other girls had been and would be in danger if the house's secrets were not exposed, that stopped her from running as far away as possible right there and then.

Just at that moment she caught a glimpse of a silver-grey Mercedes, a car she recognised instantly, and she ducked into a little-strewn alleyway opposite a set of traffic lights, pressing herself back against the crumbling outer wall of one of the shops between which the alley ran.

Poppy saw the chauffeur she'd glimpsed briefly on her arrival at the Bradburns' house, and she held her breath and tried to mould further into the wall as she recognised the profile of Lady Bradburn sitting in the back of the limo, next to a shadowy figure the gender let alone the identity of which she could not be certain.

As the lights changed to green and the car pulled effortlessly away from them, Poppy scurried out of the alley and dashed with a hammering heart back along Snode Avenue towards the house. She instantly found the barely detectable gap through the fir hedge, crept urgently but as quietly as possible through the shrubs to the small patio, unlocked the French windows and slipped silently back inside her apartment.

Instantly she hid both keys under the sink in the kitchenette with the money, changed back into her white blouse and black skirt, returning her own clothes to the trunk, and sat in one of the armchairs with a book, working hard to slow her breathing to normal and look as relaxed as she could. She had barely opened the book when she heard Lady Bradburn's voice in the hall outside, getting louder and then receding as she breezed through to another part of the house.

Poppy went quickly to the apartment door and put her ear to it, listening for any movement outside, and was relieved that she was apparently to be left alone for some time at least, allowing her a little more time to think.

While she tried to do just that she made herself a sandwich and a mug of tea, and she'd just finished the snack when the door to the apartment did open and Lady Bradburn swept in.

'Hello, ma'am,' Poppy said, thinking it might be wise to humour the woman.

'Ah, Cavendish,' Lady Bradburn said imperiously, acknowledging Poppy's greeting with a curt nod, then giving the girl a piercing stare. 'I've had a stressful day, so I think you'll do nicely to help me unwind and take my mind off matters.' She paused dramatically to let her words sink in. 'Now, come with me.'

With a haughty toss of her head Lady Bradburn turned on her heel without looking back. Poppy followed her purposeful form out into the hall, and to her dismay the woman led her to the murky corridor beneath the main staircase. They stopped outside a door that Poppy had previously found to be locked during her brief exploration.

Lady Bradburn hammered on it with her fist, there was the sound of a hefty bolt being drawn, and then the door opened and Poppy was ushered inside. At first she was surprised to see the chauffeur standing there, then fear made her mouth go dry as her wide, innocent eyes took in the leg-irons and handcuffs, straps and chains, articles of bizarre rubber clothing and hideous implements that hung from the ceiling in serried rows.

'Remove her underwear, Bradley,' she ordered the chauffeur, with barely a pause for Poppy to absorb fully what she was seeing.

'Yes, ma'am,' he responded, and Poppy was startled by the rapid change of events as the man put his hands up her skirt and snatched down her knickers, making her step out of them and then taking the opportunity to secrete them in his pocket.

'You little trollop,' Lady Bradburn said vehemently and unfairly to Poppy, clearly enjoying abusing her verbally, then lifted her short skirt up over her buttocks to verify her state of nakedness beneath it, holding the black material around her waist. 'Bradley, spank her for being such an incorrigible little tease,' she ordered.

'Very good, ma'am,' the chauffeur said, and he grabbed her wrist with one hand and used his free right hand to smack her silky cheeks, the hard smacks resounding like pistol shots in the small dank room.

'Enough,' Lady Bradburn said, stepping in as Poppy burst into tears. Then the pain of her reddening cheeks had to compete with a sudden surge of fear as Lady Bradburn ordered, 'Strip her naked, put her into collar and cuffs, and secure her hands behind her neck.'

As Bradley roughly pulled off Poppy's blouse, the buttons bursting and a few of them spilling onto the dusty floor, the harshness of the assault making her breasts quiver enticingly within the lacy white bra, Lady Bradburn induced a tremor of pleasure between the girl's legs by catching and squeezing her nipples so hard that she almost squealed, then running her hands tenderly over her encased breasts.

'Now I want to show these beauties off to their best advantage,' she said, and then tugged the bra, making the girl squeal with shock as she ripped it off with ease.

'Please!' Poppy begged as Bradley ripped the skirt off. 'Please! Why are you doing this to me?'

'Shall I put her into shackles too, ma'am?' Bradley asked, totally ignoring the girl, as though they could not hear her, fastening a black leather collar around her neck.

'Good idea, Bradley.' Lady Bradburn nodded approvingly as her servant buckled straps around their victim's slender wrists. 'Put her into a straight leg-iron, I think. I want to see her hobble.'

While Bradley fetched the correct implement, Lady Bradburn clipped Poppy's wrists to a metal ring at the back of her neck. The girl sobbed, as much from the realisation that she was enjoying the manner in which she was being treated as from the indignity, and when Lady Bradburn cupped and squeezed her outthrust breasts again she felt a knot of pleasure in the pit of her stomach that made her degradation complete.

Bradley returned with a metal bar with rings attached to its ends, and as he forced Poppy's legs apart and locked the cold steel around her ankles, the girl tried a last, desperate plea for mercy.

'Ma'am, please...' Tears brimmed from her eyes, hung momentarily in her lashes then trickled down her cheeks. 'Please let me go.'

'Nonsense, girl,' Lady Bradburn scoffed, 'you're loving every second of this, and don't try to tell me otherwise. All this comes naturally to you. You are a submissive, I know.' Then without another word she lowered her face to take one of Poppy's disloyally erect nipples between her teeth, and nipped each so painfully that her victim squealed and cringed, trying to ignore the pulse of pleasure between her legs.

'Mmmm...' the domineering woman whispered, 'time for us to be alone, I do believe.' Without taking her eyes from Poppy's she addressed her chauffeur. 'Thank you, Bradley, you may go.'

'Yes ma'am.' As the chauffeur left the room he cast Poppy a look so strangely unfathomable that she could not tell if it was born of desire or pity.

'Come here, and be quick about it,' Lady Bradburn ordered, teasingly moving away from Poppy, and despite her employer's obvious impatience, Poppy's progress was slow. The rigid bar held her legs so widely apart that she could only move forward one stiff footstep at a time, and her wrists fastened behind her neck certainly didn't help matters.

'Come along, come along,' Lady Bradburn urged, clapping her hands impatiently. 'If you don't get a move on you'll be punished, it's as simple as that.'

She almost certainly would be anyway, Poppy thought ruefully as she made her way laboriously towards the woman, with the iron rings chafing her ankles and her raised arms making her shoulders ache.

Lady Bradburn opened a second door as Poppy eventually reached her. 'Remain there and I will be back soon,' the woman told her.

Left alone again Poppy waited, wondering what lay in store for her now. She had to try and get her head around everything that was happening to her, and exactly what she was going to do about it. She began to wish she'd gone to the police when she had the chance, when she was free in Burchester, but what could she tell them? That she'd overheard part of a private telephone conversation about kidnap and slavery? That she was being held against her will by the Bradburns in their house? The fact that she was not locked in the house and was in fact in the police station able to make such an allegation would have suggested to them it was indeed a load of nonsense. They'd probably humour her, and then pat her on the head and send her on her way.

A good ten minutes passed before Lady Bradburn appeared, wearing a white medical-type coat again, as seemed to be her penchant. She walked past Poppy as though the girl was of so little value it was not worth acknowledging her, then reached back to seize her collar and dragged her to another door. She opened one button of her surgical white coat, and Poppy glimpsed the steel key-chain fixed around her naked waist before she withdrew it and turned a key in the lock.

'Stand in the corner,' she ordered when she had dragged her inside, and as Poppy meekly obeyed Lady Bradburn stood close behind her, and she must have opened her white coat because when she pressed her body against Poppy's the girl felt her bare breasts warm against her back, the nipples hard as berries.

'I don't want you telling tales to Sir Neville,' Lady Bradburn warned, 'so whilst we're having this little bit of fun together you're going to wear this.' She took a black cloth from her pocket and wound it tightly around Poppy's eyes, blocking out every hint of daylight.

'Now I'm going to enjoy myself,' the woman whispered huskily, and her hands crept around the front of Poppy's body and gently cupped and stroked her breasts, dragging her fingernails over the nipples so that the girl, locked in a world of darkness that disorientated her, flinched as she anticipated the spiteful pinching, which didn't actually materialise.

As Lady Bradburn's cool hands descended over her smooth flanks and tummy with a firmer pressure, their expertise provoked pleasure to increase and glow. By the time her fingers reached Poppy's pussy it was brimming with a warm, seeping fluid, and this made tiny liquid sounds as Lady Bradburn ran a fingertip over the girl's clitoris and probed the tight entrance to her vagina. As Poppy's shapely bottom began to move back and forth with the increase of her pleasure, Lady Bradburn closed the girl's outer lips in the gentle scissors of two fingers.

Lady Bradburn's hands moved again, one caressing Poppy's lower belly, the other burrowing between her parted legs from the rear. As the hand at her front rhythmically squeezed her sex lips its partner sought out the entrance to her little rear entrance, and Poppy lacked the temerity to ask her employer to remove the blindfold so she could watch the hands at work. She could not help wondering, though, how it was that Lady Bradburn's caress was not only much less gentle than before, but their texture also far less soft, and even a little rough. But even so, Poppy soon found herself being carried higher and higher on a rising wave of sexual joy.

'Do you like what I'm doing, Cavendish?' Lady Bradburn asked sweetly in her ear.

'I-I do, it's lovely, ma'am,' the girl replied with candour.

'And what about *this?*' a male voice demanded, making Poppy's blood run cold, unexpected pain scalding her buttocks as a cruel hand smacked both her buttocks in turn.

'C-Captain Smythe?' Poppy asked, bursting into renewed tears as she realised the nature of the trick that had been played on her. Lady Bradburn laughed cruelly and seized her breasts again.

'On your knees!' the captain commanded, placing his hands on Poppy's shoulders and pushing her down to the floor. 'I'm disappointed with you, Cavendish. I stuck my neck out when I recommended you for this post, now it seems you've fallen down on the job.'

'Oh!' Pain made Poppy gasp as her knees hit the floor, for the bar that held her feet apart put a terrific strain on her legs. 'Sir, I don't know what you mean?'

Her words were promptly smothered as the captain's erect penis wedged into her mouth, only to be supplanted by hot, slippery female flesh as Lady Bradburn thrust her hips forward and pushed him out of the way. After that Poppy was conscious only of being used to satisfy the pair's lusts as they rubbed their sexual organs greedily across her startled features, and as the selfishness of their movements made her heart quicken with surreptitious delight she felt a renewed pleasure arise from between her legs, stronger now and impossible to ignore.

At that moment Poppy realised a terrible truth about herself; that as much as she wanted to push the lascivious couple away and rip off the blindfold, a large part of her also wanted to stay forever in a world of submissiveness. Resignedly she opened her mouth and began to lick and suck, at the same time murmuring her mounting excitement. Wishing her hands were not clamped behind her neck so that she could sneak a finger between her legs to her own swimming pussy, she moved her hips back and forth with gathering lust. When one of her tormentors placed a naked leg in front of her she rubbed her cunt against it gratefully, the humiliating degradation of the act making her spiral ever faster towards orgasm. Then just when she was sure she would come at any second, the leg was withdrawn and the humid flesh left her face.

Captain Smythe began grunting and groaning in the throes of animal passion, and even if Lady Bradburn had not cried her encouragement the squelching of wet flesh upon wet flesh would have told Poppy what was going on. The captain and Lady Bradburn were fucking, she knew, realising now why the pair had made her wear the blindfold.

As though reading her thoughts, Captain Smythe croaked, 'Shall I punish her,

Lady Bradburn, until she makes a vow of silence?'

'Yes!' the woman cried, though whether in answer to his question or as an expression of growing passions Poppy could not tell. The sound of flesh grinding against flesh abated as the lustful couple drew apart, and Poppy's keen ears listened intently as the man moved away. He returned at once, and the girl began to squeal anew as an unseen instrument of correction cut the air.

Swish!

'Oh sir, *please*, not the cane!' she begged, tears of anguish seeping out from beneath the blindfold and dripping from her chin onto the smooth upper slopes of her outthrust breasts, which quivered enticingly under the influence of her staccato breathing. 'I'll do anything if you spare me the cane!'

Swish!

The cane cut the air harmlessly but threateningly in what must have been a practice shot, because a moment later Poppy began to howl hopelessly as the thin, cruel bamboo striped the redness of her spanked bottom.

'That's enough for the present,' Lady Bradburn announced, and Poppy knew that the pair had begun fucking again when she heard them groaning as their bodies moved audibly in the darkness. Soon Lady Bradburn's, and then the captain's hands began mauling Poppy's body in an orgy of selfish greed. As one of them, so confused was she that she had no idea who, squeezed her breasts and pinched her nipples, the other stroked the smooth valley between her buttocks, and although this was unsettling in the total darkness it was also immensely exciting. When one hand slid against her pussy to test its brimming wetness while another rubbed the tiny bud of flesh that protruded there, Poppy began to moan and pant as loudly as her tormentors.

'The depraved little creature's close to having an orgasm,' Lady Bradburn panted, when she noticed their victim's body was contorting in passion as well as pain. 'Stop that at once, you lascivious girl.'

Swipe!

Poppy guessed that Lady Bradburn was the one wielding the vicious cane this time, and the pain it induced made her moan and pant even more desperately than the pleasure had done moments earlier. Her intuition was confirmed when the blows finally ceased and she heard the cane being dropped to the floor at her feet, for the mouth and chin that were thrust between her open legs then could only have belonged to a woman.

As Lady Bradburn's tongue began working furiously on Poppy's pussy, Captain Smythe moved behind the panting girl. He reached around her body, squeezed her breasts, and slid his stiff penis between her legs from the rear, where it slid back and forth between her buttocks and against her sex lips.

Lady Bradburn began to moan excitedly and the captain to groan ever louder, and when Poppy realised that her employer was sucking the ex-military man's seeping cock-head with every forward thrust, she began to rise with them to unstoppable heights of pleasure. Lady Bradburn must have been fingering herself madly while this was going on, because her moans and cries grew rhythmically louder with those of the other two.

When the inevitable emission of hot, slippery liquid ejaculated from Captain Smyth's rigid member into Lady Bradburn's mouth and over her face, she used her tongue to spread it over Poppy's clitoral area, so that all three of them gasped and threshed in the excitement of a simultaneous orgasm.

It took some time for their intense passions to subside, but when it finally did so Lady Bradburn removed Poppy's blindfold while Captain Smythe released her ankles from the leg-irons. Then carrying the horrible implement in one hand and his clothes in the other, he left the room, still naked and without uttering another word, while Lady Bradburn surprised Poppy by kissing her long and hard on the lips.

'You're not going to tell anyone about what happened here today, are you, Cavendish?'

'Of course not, ma'am,' Poppy said sincerely, having no desire whatsoever to get into any more trouble than she was already in. 'I wouldn't do that.'

'Good girl,' said the woman, apparently happy with the girl's response. 'Now, I'm going to ask you an important question, and I want a truthful answer.' The woman gave her a probing stare before going on. 'In the short time since you've been with us, have you seen anything that would make you believe my husband is being unfaithful?'

'No, ma'am!' Poppy felt a crimson blush rising over her cheeks as she told the lie. Lying was alien to Poppy, but she felt a need to elaborate upon it. 'How could I? How could I when I've only spent such a short time here and barely been allowed out of my apartment anyway?'

'What about Jessop?' Lady Bradburn persisted.

'Jessop, ma'am?' Poppy continued to look bemused by the line of questioning, rather pleasing herself with her performance. 'She's the housemaid, ma'am, that's all I know.'

Lady Bradburn seemed content with Poppy's responses, removed the bondage accessories, then took her back to the apartment and locked her in, and life in the house reverted to normal, if normal is a word that could be applied to a place where sexual excesses seemed commonplace.

The throbbing in Poppy's caned buttocks meant that she slept that night on her front.

The next morning Lucy Jessop came bustling in early, banging and stomping around Poppy's small apartment, vacuuming and dusting and generally making it impossible for Poppy to remain in bed.

So she got up, and having showered she padded back into her bedroom just as the maid was reaching up on tiptoe to swipe away a cobweb in one corner, her skirt rising as she stretched and allowing Poppy to see that her bottom, too, was scored red as the result of a thorough caning.

'Lucy?' Without thinking Poppy reached out and touched the weals that scored the upper region of one buttock, making the maid wince. 'Why have you been punished?'

The girl cast her a vicious glare. 'For some reason Lady Bradburn seems to thing I've been fucking her husband,' she said vehemently and crudely.

'Well I didn't tell her such a thing,' Poppy replied defensively. 'How could I know if you have or you haven't been, um, *fucking* Sir Neville?' The coarse word sounded strange coming from her own lips.

The maid nodded slowly at this, and seemed less belligerent as she told the girl to lie down on the bed so she could perform her duty of anointing the stripes that crisscrossed Poppy's bare bottom.

When she'd performed this duty again and finished her cleaning she seemed to have released her earlier anger, and with Poppy dressed in her white blouse and black skirt there was a knock on the door. Lucy opened it and let in a young man who, it turned out, was there to carry out a routine safety check on the apartment's gas fittings - the fire in the small lounge, the water heater in the bathroom and the oven in the kitchenette.

As he opened his toolbox Lucy gathered up her cleaning equipment and left to carry on her chores in the rest of the vast house, leaving Poppy and the young man alone. As Poppy wondered if she would be summoned by Sir Neville or Lady Bradburn, or both of them, she could not help casting furtive glances at the handsome blond worker, whistling cheerfully as he toiled.

Wanting to engage in conversation with someone from the outside world, and finding him actually very attractive, she offered him a cup of coffee. He accepted, and when she'd made it they talked together for a while in the tiny kitchen, remarkably easy in each other's company. He cracked a few jokes and they laughed together, Poppy nearly melting when he smiled broadly at her, his eyes sparkling mischievously.

Eventually she gathered her courage to ask his name, albeit rather clumsily.

'Tony,' he told her. He moved to place his empty coffee mug on the work surface, and for a moment their hands touched and they looked intently at each other, Poppy longing to reach up and give him a gentle kiss.

'Tonight,' he said cryptically.

'I beg your pardon?' Poppy whispered.

'Tonight,' he repeated, 'meet me tonight, by the bridge in town.'

Poppy absolutely longed to slip away from the house to meet him, but she dared not. 'No, I... I can't,' she said sadly. 'Don't ask why, I just can't.'

'Yes, you can,' he insisted, Poppy finding his naturally positive attitude incredibly endearing and uplifting, and very difficult to say no to. 'I'll be there anyway, waiting for you, at nine o'clock.'

And then he had packed up his tools, hoisted up his heavy toolbox in a strong hand, and gone, quietly closing the apartment door behind him.

Alone again, Poppy slumped into one of the armchairs and tried to evaluate what was going on in her life and how she was going to deal with it. She knew she could make an attempt to run away, but she had nowhere to go and no one to go to, and she also had little doubt the combined influences of Maidenhall and the Bradburns would track her down and bring her back, and she would almost certainly find herself in an even worse predicament than she was currently in - bad though that was.

She also felt strongly that she had a mission to find out as much as she could about what exactly was going on at the house, and where Maidenhall fitted into the grand scheme of things. If other girls were finding themselves embroiled in some despicable people smuggling ring, or if innocent girls might in the future, then she felt a strong duty to do what she could to expose the whole loathsome operation.

Then she thought about Tony, his physical appeal and his fresh-faced wholesomeness.

She wanted nothing more than to slip into town that evening and meet him by the bridge, but she dared not... or did she?

At five minutes past nine Poppy hurried along Snode Avenue towards the town and the bridge. The evening was pleasantly balmy, but despite that there were few people out and about, for which she was grateful.

She feared she'd be too late and Tony would think she wasn't coming and would amble off somewhere else, probably to be chatted up by some other girl or girls in one of the local pubs. He was certainly cute enough to attract attention from others.

But turning the last corner she saw the bridge... and there he was, waiting for her right in the middle of it, leaning on the ornate stone balustrade and idly dropping broken bits of twig into the meandering water below. Her chest tightened when she saw him, as handsome as she remembered him to be. Without noticing her approaching he checked his wristwatch once, so she hurried on towards him.

'Hi!' she called as she neared, smiling tentatively.

'Hi.' He beamed a smile that made her legs go momentarily weak, standing up straight and turning towards her.

Then all thought and speech took flight from Poppy's head and lips respectively, and she stood before him searching desperately for something to say, feeling utterly foolish and awkward. Tony didn't seem to be fairing too much better, which surprised her because he had been so confident earlier.

But after a few minutes saying how nice the other looked, and commenting on what a pleasant evening it was, Tony suggested they go for a relaxing stroll along the riverbank.

'I can't be late, though,' Poppy told him reluctantly, although she didn't elaborate on why not, leaving him to assume what he would, probably that her job description included a time when she had to be in at night. 'I must get back at a sensible time. I can't risk being out too long.'

'Sure,' he grinned, in his usual cheeky, effervescent manner that Poppy was finding increasingly endearing, 'no problem. I'll make sure you get home safe and sound.'

Poppy wanted to confide in him that she didn't really have a home, and where she was presently certainly was not her home, but she held back; that could wait until she knew him that little bit better, and she didn't want to dampen the pleasant mood that already existed between them.

Eventually, as they wandered along the grassy towpath in the peaceful evening, Tony pointed to a tumbledown cottage beyond a ramshackle little jetty, beneath a beautiful old weeping willow.

'I've bought that place, Poppy, and I'm going to do it up and live there,' he told her. 'It's my ideal place. My own little sanctuary away from the madness of the outside world. What do you think?'

'Oh, it's beautiful, Tony,' she beamed with genuine enthusiasm. 'Can we take a look inside?'

'Course we can,' he said. 'I was hoping you'd want to.' She followed him along the path to the rickety front door of the cottage, where he stopped and turned, catching her by complete surprise, and took her in his arms and kissed her, a long, deep kiss that grew increasingly passionate, leaving Poppy shocked and breathless.

'Oh,' was all she could say, blushing furiously when the kiss finally ended.

'The floor's a bit dodgy just inside the doorway,' he said, looking a little bashful and carrying on as though he'd not just done what he had just done. As he opened the reluctant and loudly creaking front door, Poppy could see it was dark within the dilapidated old building, so she was glad when he took her hand and they carefully ducked under the low doorway and step inside.

'Here,' he said from the impenetrable gloom, 'give me your other hand too, there's an old oil lamp and some matches over here...'

Poppy had no sooner offered her other hand than there was a double metallic click and the door was kicked shut, cutting off what little light was able to seep into the dingy little cottage.

'Got her!' he cried exultantly. 'Told you I would, didn't I lads? Told you I'd get her!'

Chapter 7

Poppy was speechless, blinking as a dim light filled the cottage. At first she was so disorientated that she found it impossible to comprehend the scene before her, but when she did she burst into tears. 'Don't tell me you've betrayed me,' she eventually managed to wail in horror, 'after everything you said!'

And she knew he had done just that as her eyes grew accustomed to the gloom and she saw Bradley, the Bradburns' chauffeur, sitting on a grubby old sofa with another male, whose long hair and broad build told her it was their gardener.

Poppy looked down at her hands, and her stomach turned a somersault at the sight of them locked in a pair of metal cuffs. As she tugged at them feebly, hurting her tender wrists inside the rings of uncompromising steel, Bradley and his friend put down the cans of beer they were holding, stood up, and without ceremony began to slowly unzip their flies. Unable to believe what was happening to her, and realising she was at their mercy, Poppy tried desperately to stave off the exquisite impulse of surrender. Perverse feelings of bliss threatened to engulf her, vying with the instinct to stand up to them.

'I don't know what you think you're doing, luring me here like this,' she said in her most assertive voice, 'but you'd better be aware of one thing.' She paused and drew her shoulders back defiantly. 'If you don't unlock these handcuffs and open that door at once, I'll make sure you spend the next ten years walking from the cell block to the exercise yard!'

The most spectacular effect of Poppy having her back ramrod-straight was that it made her breasts thrust even more enticingly than ever. The gardener's eyes latched on to them hungrily, quickly followed by his hands and outstretched fingers, roughened and calloused from his work. At the same time Bradley and Tony caressed her bottom, neatly encased in her tight jeans.

'Always the tit man, eh Dave?' Bradley chuckled, and slipped his fingertips into the cleft that separated the cheeks of Poppy's shapely bottom, tracing the narrow vertical seam of denim that nestled snugly between them.

Aware that she should have found the experience frightening and shocking, Poppy experienced a guilty thrill instead. Tony's fingers had moved around to her front and were rubbing her sex mound through the denim. 'Each to his own, Bradley,' he said. 'Each to his own.'

Then Poppy squealed unconvincingly as those same fingers un-popped the brass stud button at her waist, and at the same time the gardener grinned lecherously as he tugged her T-shirt out of her jeans and tantalisingly rolled it up towards her breasts.

Everything seemed to happen so fast then, and in no time she was naked, lying on the grimy floorboards, Bradley's stiff cock pressing against one buttock while the gardener rubbed the wet tip of his bloated cock against her thigh. Tony slipped a finger between her legs, and found her brimming with feminine juices.

'Your pussy says it all, love,' he goaded her. 'You're enjoying every second of this.' Then with his eyes locked on hers, challenging her to deny the truth of what he said, he wiped his wet finger slowly over her nipples so that they gleamed in the half-light. 'And to show you we're nice blokes really, we'll let you choose,' he said with apparent generosity. 'Which of us do you want to fuck first?'

He knelt up over her, grinning his boyish grin, and despite her conflicting emotions she looked up curiously as he too pulled his cock out. To her wide, secretly appreciative eyes it was perfectly proportioned, and as he fed its bulbous head between her legs and rubbed it forward and back, forward and back, an overwhelming sensation of pleasure radiated throughout her body from her sex.

'All of you,' she whispered shamefully.

'What?' Tony cruelly teased. 'Say that again; the lads didn't quite catch it.'

'All of you,' she repeated, knowing he was intentionally toying with her and enjoying watching her humiliation.

'There you go, lads,' he beamed. 'She's telling us to help ourselves.'

'But don't fuck her,' Bradley warned. 'If we did and old Bradburn found out she'd be straight on the warpath. Our lives wouldn't be worth living. What we're doing is bad enough.'

'Okay,' Tony said after a short, reflective silence. 'We won't fuck her tonight.'

'Agreed,' said the gardening, obviously rating his job highly.

The three randy men fell upon her then in an orgy of uncontrolled lust. Tony fastened his lips on hers and kissed her fervently. Bradley held the distended tip of his heavy organ in his fist, rubbing first her pussy and then her anus as the gardener was kissing and groping her breasts with fanatical hunger.

A surge of intense pleasure radiated from her pussy, and Poppy gave herself up to its lure. She ground her hips over Bradley's stiff penis so that the sensations of both were heightened, at the same time pushing her shapely breasts into Dave's face, encouraging him to suck avidly.

As Tony's hand returned to her pussy, where its middle finger stroked her stiffening clitoris, her tongue rolled around his with dizzying intensity.

'Please, take these off,' she panted, indicating the cuffs.

'Okay,' Tony said calculatingly, 'if that's what you want.' But then he nodded at a battered old coffee table in the middle of the room with a jerk of his thumb. 'Let's tie her down on that, lads.'

With murmurs of agreement they carried and pulled her into a star shape, tied her wrists and ankles with ropes looped around the tops of the short table legs, and fell upon her again in orgiastic greed.

Driven by an intensity of desire that surprised even her, and despite being virtually immobilised by the ropes, Poppy gave as good as she got. She twisted her body into every rabid caress and licked and sucked anything that came near her mouth. She groaned and panted desperately as excitement took her higher and higher.

Tony then squatted behind her and directed his cock downwards and forward until he sank deep into her mouth, when he began grinding back and forth, fucking her upturned face. The gardener latched his mouth to her pussy, his tongue tantalising her stiff clitoris, and as this torment was going on a rigid finger circled her anus until she began to moan and buck, then it drove inside her rear passage all the way up to the knuckle.

After a while they all moved round, and a delirious Poppy managed to lift her head to see Dave's fat erection disappearing between her buttocks, penetrating her there. The thrill she felt as it entered her bottom and sank in further and further, stretching her as it progressed and seemed to grow fatter, was nothing compared to her excitement when Tony opened the lips of her pussy and started to tongue her clitoris and vagina.

Soon all four bodies, three male and one female, were bucking and threshing in a rhythm that grew ever more frantic, while the moans and cries of the sexually active quartet grew louder and more abandoned.

Tony grunted, the noise betraying his closeness to an orgasm. Dave's cock was embedded in her bottom to the hilt, with the result that Poppy was sobbing with discomfort and pleasure combined as his heavy scrotum rocked against her buttocks. Bradley giving her clitoris a fervent tongue-lashing sent Poppy into rapture, and she craftily reached down and began to pump his cock. She lay stranded on the very borderlands of an orgasm as Tony passed through it, sinking his fat cock deep as copious amounts of seed erupted from its tip.

Bradley groaned desperately as Poppy's rapid friction of his cock sent him towards a precipice of pleasure, and she gazed through dreamy eyes as he shifted onto his knees and ejaculated all over her breasts.

Dave made a guttural noise too, and then Poppy felt his warm seed pumping deep into her bottom.

When Poppy slipped back into her apartment feeling exhausted, aching, and most of all betrayed by Tony, her hopes of them falling for each other completely shattered, her illusions of what a lovely young man he was crushed, she was shocked to find Lucy perched on one of the armchairs, sobbing quietly into a tissue, a box of them on the floor by her feet.

Her initial reaction was the fear that her clandestine forays into the outside world had been discovered, but then it was clear the maid was in some distress over something and more distracted with her own problems than Poppy's illicit activities, so she sat on the arm of the chair and put a comforting arm around her shoulder.

'What's the matter?' she asked.

'Lady Bradburn gave me a *real* ticking off because she knows now for certain that Sir Neville has been carrying on with me behind her back,' the girl wailed pitifully, letting it all out without pausing.

'What did she do?' Poppy pressed, certain that it must have been pretty severe to upset the brash maid so much. 'Did she beat you again?'

The maid blew her nose in the tissue, which was by now pretty soggy. 'Oh no,' she sniffled. 'If that was all I could handle it, no problem. You should know by now how much I enjoy a good healthy thrashing.'

Poppy nodded, suspecting that to be true. 'So what did she do?'

'It wasn't so much what she *did*,' Lucy told her, 'but what she *said*.'

'Oh? So what did she say?'

'She said that she would have to carefully consider my future, and that there was every chance she would dispense with my services!' Lucy started crying and sniffling again, burying her face in a fresh tissue tugged from the box. 'I've been here for three years and I don't want to have to leave. I've nowhere to go, and no friends or family.'

For the first time Poppy's heart went out to the girl, understanding exactly how she felt because their lives seemed sadly similar. 'I'm sure you'll be okay,' she tried to reassure the maid, whose previously belligerent bearing had dissolved completely and all Poppy now saw was a very insecure and fragile female.

'But you don't understand,' Lucy said. 'If she does get rid of me that would be terrible enough, but she also threatened that I would go the same way as the other girls and be...' Lucy's voice tailed off, as she clearly realised she'd probably said far too much already.

'Sold abroad?' Poppy carefully probed, seeing a chance to get some confirmation of her suspicions.

Lucy stopped snivelling and looked up at her carefully. 'Yes,' she ventured, 'sold abroad. How do you know that?'

'It's okay,' Poppy said comfortingly, 'I overheard a telephone conversation Sir Neville had with some guy called Hamid. He sounded like a real creep?'

'He *is*.'

Poppy wasn't surprised to receive such fervent confirmation of this. 'And I think I know what's going on here. Perhaps I'm not as stupid as some might think.'

'I really don't know why she's being so horrible to me,' Lucy carried on, bringing the subject back to her woes. 'I've always been a hard worker, and loyal to her beyond the cause. And it's not as if *she's* perfectly loyal to *him*.'

'No?' This comment interested Poppy. Was she about to learn something that could be used to her benefit?

'No. She's been unfaithful to Sir Neville ever since I can remember,' the maid disclosed.

'She has? With whom?'

'Well, Captain Smythe, of course. And it's not exactly a big secret. Heaven knows how Sir Neville feels about it, poor bloke.'

'Really...?' Poppy mused, tapping her chin as she thought about this revelation, although it wasn't that much of a surprise to have her strong suspicions confirmed as correct.

And then she remembered the way she had briefly mistaken Robert Bradburn for Captain Smythe when she saw him standing outside her French window that first night... 'So Lady Bradburn and Captain Smythe have been a long-term item, eh?'

The following morning Poppy felt a strong need to slip into Burchester, to the post office, to check if Karen had replied to her letter. As soon as she got a chance she would have to try to sneak away from the house.

As she ate a slice of toast for breakfast she looked out of the French windows, firstly gazing wistfully at the perimeter hedge beyond the shrubs, and then noticing something protruding under the door, having been pushed through from the outside. It was a sealed white envelope, with her name scrawled on it. She opened it and read.

I'm sorry for last night. Meet me in the Russian Literature section of Burchester library at 10 a.m. - T.

It was from Tony! Poppy felt an involuntary glow as she thought of him, despite the fact he'd turned out to be a complete rat!

Why did he want to see her? Did he have something to say to her? Poppy just had to find out, no matter that in doing so she'd be taking a huge risk of being discovered with a key and therefore a means of getting away - if she chose to do that instead of trying to hijack the despicable trade being perpetrated from behind the façade of the respectable and respected house and its residents. It was unlikely, but perhaps Tony wanted to make amends for the way he'd duped her and had some information that might help in her plans. And perhaps she could get to the post office while she was out, and see if Karen had written. She really hoped her friend had.

She quickly dressed in her jeans and T-shirt again, looking stunningly attractive as she escaped the confines of her apartment again and made it into town.

Soon she trotted up the steps of the redbrick building, passed a brass plate that read, *Burchester Library*, and through a double door into the reference section, where even a muted cough caused brows to furrow and lips to purse behind stiffly raised forefingers. She thought how much she loved the studious atmosphere of the place, its peaceful quiet, its smell of polished floorboards and old books.

She found Russian Literature at the far end of the long, capacious room, but its crowded shelves seemed devoid of any other human interest whatsoever. She checked her watch - it was bang on ten o'clock - so she wondered what to do next. Was Tony still playing silly games on her after all?

Poppy waited in the library for a full half hour, and then, concerned about being away from the house for so long at such a dangerous time of day, she decided Tony was indeed a complete rat - and an immature one at that for playing such a childish prank on her on top of what he'd previously done with his randy cohorts.

Feeling extremely flat that someone she thought she liked could behave so badly towards her yet again, and feeling silly for being made such a fool of by his note, she decided to nip into the post office to check on a possible reply from Karen, and then head back to the house as quickly as she could, before her presence was missed.

There was indeed a reply from Karen, and Poppy's spirits lifted immeasurably as she left the post office and tore the letter open whilst quickly retracing her steps.

Dear Poppy

Thanks for the letters. I got them the other day. Poppy, something terrible has happened. My guardian back in the States is trying to cheat me out of my inheritance. You may find this hard to believe, but Suky Desai thinks that Maidenhall is conspiring to help him. I don't agree, as Captain Smythe and Old Sharpie have offered me some help by finding me a job with a respected couple in Burchester. I think Suky is going there, too, but she's suspicious about the whole deal. What do you think we should do?

Try to write and let me know.

Karen

Poppy knew things were bad, but now the situation was worse than ever. The fact that Karen and Suky were being lined up for a spell with the Bradburns meant that they were earmarked for Hamid too, and that Poppy herself would soon be 'despatched' to make room for them, which meant that time was running out fast. Panic gripped her. As Poppy absorbed the words and then reread them for a second and then a third time she was aware of little else around her, and it wasn't until she actually bumped into the person that she looked up, ready to deliver an apology for not looking where she was going. But when she did look up she gave a little squeal of shock and raised a hand to her open mouth.

'Well, well, well, if it isn't our little Poppy Cavendish,' Robert Bradburn said with a wolfish grin. 'Hello, my dear girl. What on earth are you doing out and about by yourself?'

Chapter 8

It was almost as if he was expecting to bump into her, Poppy thought as Robert blocked her way with his bulk and an unpleasant smile, then backed her into a deserted alley. It was as though it had been prearranged. As if she'd been set up. By Tony?

The disconcerted girl had no way of knowing it, but from that moment her luck would slowly change for the better. The first sign of this came when Robert was distracted by a car horn nearby, and as he impatiently looked over his shoulder to see what the noise was all about, Poppy had the wherewithal to snatch the opportunity to screw up Karen's letter and drop it to the ground, and use her heel to nudge it amongst all the other rotting litter strewn around their feet.

'I don't suppose my mother knows you've been getting out?' he said, backing her further into the alley, well out of sight of the street, pushing her up against a damp and crumbling old brick wall.

'Please don't tell her.' Terror at the thought that he might do just that gripped Poppy's heart.

'I do hope you weren't thinking of running to the authorities, with some flighty story or other about kidnap and slave trading.'

'N-no, why should I?' She did her best to look up at him with wide, innocent eyes, as though completely confused by his words.

He studied her face closely, gauging her reaction to the intentional hint he'd dropped, clearly trying to ascertain if she knew more than she should. 'Both my parents are magistrates, and we have very good friends in the police force. Just you remember that.'

'Yes, I will.'

'Come on,' he said, seemingly satisfied with her response. 'I have to see a man about a dog, and I'm already late. But I fancy a little fun first, and if you're nice to me I might just forget to tell my parents I bumped into you. On the other hand, if you're not nice it might just be the first thing I tell them when I get home later...'

He started to move against her, squashing her uncomfortably against the wall, and from his actions she knew he was undoing his trousers.

'Sir, I really should be getting back?'

'Shut up,' he said casually. 'I don't have time to mess about.' He moved Poppy's wrist and she felt his semi-erect penis being pressed into her hand. 'Give me a quick wank, and we'll say no more about what you've been up to.'

And then he placed his hands on the wall beside her shoulders and widened his stance a little. Poppy felt his cock stiffening until it was soon fully erect in her fist. He held her gaze and smiled enigmatically as she obediently began to work her hand back and forth.

'Come on,' he urged, his hips beginning to move very slightly, matching the rhythm of her arm. 'Come on, I don't want to be too late for my appointment.'

Poppy knew only too well that she was being used as nothing more than a means for him to gain quick, sordid, sexual gratification, and she loathed him for that. But she also experienced a deep, secret thrill from that very same knowledge. The thrill grew and for some perversely wicked reason she wanted to make the arrogant man ejaculate - she wanted him to come over her hand. She also wanted to get back to the house pretty sharpish so the sooner she satisfied Robert the better.

'That's good,' he said calmly, his expression giving little indication of how excited he was. 'That's very good. Just a little more, Poppy... just a little more.'

He held her gaze still, just that unfathomable smile indicating any emotion as his hips moved a little more urgently against her pumping hand. She could feel his cock pulsing more noticeably and new he was close to coming. She licked her lips and urged him on with a quiet whisper, coaxing him towards a climax with her soft words of encouragement and the soft smoothness of her palm and fingers.

She tore her eyes away from his penetrating stare and looked down, just as a thick dribble of pre-come oozed from the bulbous purple helmet protruding from her tightly clamped fingers. Then he gave a strangled hiss of release and creamy semen erupted into the air, some arcing high before splattering down onto the ground and litter, and some coating her fingers and the back of her hand.

The only other physical sign that Robert Bradburn had enjoyed Poppy's attention was his slightly heavy breathing, but even that quickly calmed. 'Very nice,' he said nonchalantly, refastening his trousers and straightening his shirt. He took a hanky from his pocket and tossed it indifferently at Poppy, and she used it to wipe her hand clear of his sticky residue. She then hesitantly offered it back to him, but with a curled lip and a nod of his head he sneeringly indicated that she should discard it with the other rotting litter.

Then he turned and headed for the exit of the alley, leaving Poppy standing there uncertainly. After a few steps he stopped and turned, took a pound coin from his trouser pocket, and with his thumb he flicked it into the air towards her. It caught the light for a moment before landing on the ground, where it rolled and then spun for a few seconds, before running out of momentum and coming to a halt where it lay.

'Don't spend it all at once,' he sniggered scornfully. 'And get yourself home before I change my mind and tell my parents after all.'

A few hours later the door to Poppy's apartment was unlocked and opened, and Sir Neville entered.

'Ah, Cavendish, my dear,' he said, seeing Poppy sitting thoughtfully in one of the armchairs, gazing out of the French window, deep in thought about duplicitous people and what she was going to do about them. If he knew she was making the final decision that she simply had to make her escape that night he would not have smiled at her with such a twinkle in his eye and a lecherous grin on his lips. Or perhaps he would, for that knowledge would have given him the perfect excuse to give her a thorough spanking.

Not that he needed any excuse to give her a thorough spanking.

His eyes travelled up her crossed legs to where her thighs disappeared into her black skirt, paused at her shapely hips, and rose to linger at her mouth-watering breasts inside her white blouse.

'What are you doing, my dear?' he asked, closing the door and then moving to sit in the vacant armchair, without ever taking his greedy eyes from her.

'Nothing very much, sir,' she answered truthfully.

He leaned forward and patted her knee, letting his cold hand linger there, making no attempt to remove it but gently squeezing and stroking. 'Is there anything you need?' he asked, and if Poppy didn't know better she could have mistaken the query as a genuine interest in her welfare. She shook her head, watching the hand circling possessively on her knee, very gradually moving up until his fingernails disappeared under he skirt.

'Then perhaps you'd be sweet enough to make an old man very happy and let him see your delightful bottom one more time...'

One more time? Was that a significant slip of the tongue?

'Perhaps you'd stand here,' he indicated the floor directly beside his polished brogue shoes, 'and lift up your skirt so I can admire your bottom again.'

Suspecting it might be a very good idea to appease the man and lull him into a false sense of security, if she could, Poppy slowly stood up and took the two paces to his side. He looked up at her, his eyes again glinting avariciously.

One hand lifted and reached around to caress the curvaceous contours of her bottom as his eyes lowered to her breasts for a while, his lusting for her almost tangible, and then lifted again to her face.

'Very nice, my dear,' he said gruffly, and then his other hand squeezed between her thighs and the back of a knuckle rubbed softly against the gentle swell of her sex mound, closely cosseted inside her tight white knickers, the hem of her black skirt draped over the slowly moving blue forearm of his blazer. 'Very nice indeed. Now, turn around for me.'

Poppy meekly obeyed, and then waited quietly as she felt her skirt being raised and a low rumble of appreciation coming from his chest. 'Oh, my dear,' he said hungrily, 'hold your skirt up for me.' Poppy obeyed, and he used both eager hands to cup her buttocks and squeeze and caress them adoringly.

'Perhaps I shouldn't be telling you this,' he went on, 'but I really wish you could stay here...' He and the room fell silent then, save for the rasping breath that indicated the intensity of his yearning for her, and Poppy realised the man was on the point of imparting something momentous...

But then his mood changed and he sighed. 'Oh, never mind,' and Poppy bit her lip as a hand squeezed between her thighs from behind and rubbed tight against her sex lips through her white knickers, a knuckle nudging her clitoris and sending a shard of excitement spearing through her body. 'I just want you to know that I'm not necessarily like all the others,' he did add, almost to himself, almost as an afterthought, almost as an apology.

Smack!

His free hand swept down unexpectedly on her right cheek with ferocious force, Poppy rocking forward under the impact, and it had no sooner despatched its livid scalding than it meted out similar punishment to her left.

Smack!

A series of rapid blows followed, and just as the pain of the spanking was making Poppy struggle to hold back the tears, Sir Neville stopped and resumed his consuming caresses, with one thumb-tip sinking between her beaten buttocks to agitate her anus, taking her knickers with it, while the other teased her clitoris.

'You're a naughty girl, aren't you?' Sir Neville said.

'Yes sir, if that's what you think,' Poppy mumbled.

'What are you?' he demanded, stimulating her erect clitoris while his thumb penetrated her tight anus just a little way, making her gasp and nibble her lip again.

'A naughty girl, sir,' she whispered, recognising the approach of an orgasm.

'Then you must be punished,' Sir Neville pronounced. 'Move forward a little and bend over.'

Feeling simultaneously humiliated and sexy, Poppy shuffled a step or two and then reached down to grip her ankles. Then she heard the rustle of leather sliding through the loops on the waistband of his trousers, making her stomach churn with dread.

'Now I'm going to whip your bottom with my belt, young lady,' he told her, 'and when I have finished you will please me in whatever way I wish.'

'Y-yes, sir,' she whispered breathlessly.

Then to her surprise he gathered her hair in his left fist and held it like a rein as he stood to her side, the belt dangling from his right hand. There was a short pause that was strained with tension, then Poppy caught from the corner of her eye the belt being raised...

Crack! Crack! Crack!

Sounding like a volley of pistol shots, the pliable leather strap snapped down on her defenceless bottom again and again, her flimsy panties offering her no protection whatsoever. Poppy squealed each time the heavy belt struck, curling a cruel path around her tender flesh to her hip, and leaving angry bands of pain when it came away.

Poppy knew the experience had rapidly got to Sir Neville as he quickly dropped the belt aside and moved round in front of her. Pulling and adjusting her shoulders into the position he wanted, but keeping her bent forward from the waist, he lifted her chin in one hand and wasted not a second in feeding his monstrous penis between her moist and parted lips, deep into her mouth.

Despite her best intentions, she almost gagged as its considerable girth filled her and its head touched the back of her throat. Then as he began to fuck her mouth, one hand cupping her chin and one gripping her hair, her eyes widened, staring at his trousers and the small check pattern on his shirt, which moved back and forth with each increasingly agitated thrust.

Poppy gripped her knees to brace herself as his movements became more turbulent and there was a hoarse groan from above, and as her own climax took hold and her body shivered and trembled through its bliss, she felt viscous cream filling her mouth and bursting down her throat. She swallowed what she could, and Sir Neville did not seem displeased when the rest overflowed her tightly stretched lips and ran down her chin, glistening thickly.

A lull fell over the small apartment as the two gathered their thoughts, but this was rudely disrupted when the door burst open and Lady Bradburn surged in, with Bradley in close attendance.

Chapter 9

'At it again, you old goat?' she scoffed at her husband. 'You know very well she's almost due for despatch and therefore out of bounds to you. You know how our client prefers the goods to be unmarked.'

Poppy felt sickened at the woman's ominous words.

'And as for you, Cavendish,' Lady Bradburn went on, turning her imperious gaze upon the mortified girl, 'I think it's time to put you out of temptation's way. I suspected I might have to with such an attractive specimen as you. I should have followed my instincts earlier.'

Poppy was in despair. She should have got away sooner instead of trying to play the heroine. She'd had the opportunities, and now she'd surely blown it big time. She'd never get away now, and who knew what kind of a future lay in store for her?

Bradley secured an uncompromising grip on her upper arm, and led her out of the apartment to the passage beneath the stairs, soon stopping outside one of the menacing doors. As Lady Bradburn unlocked and opened it Poppy looked up at the chauffeur's stern face, looking for just a glimmer of compassion.

'Put her in collar, cuffs and anklets, Bradley,' Lady Bradburn ordered as they entered the room, the walls and ceiling of which were hung with threatening implements. The tightness of her mouth informed Poppy of her anger, and her eyes glittered as she went on, 'No more leather and buckles for you, my girl. It's going to be forged steel and padlocks from now on.'

Bradley's chest brushed against Poppy's breasts as he slipped a shiny metal collar - to be her badge of slavery - around her throat. Poppy heard its lock click with an awful finality, and when her wrists and ankles had shared a similar fate Lady Bradburn beckoned to Bradley with a crooked finger. 'Now put her in the frame.'

'Yes, ma'am,' he said with evident respect, and Poppy's knees quaked as the man led her to a circle of steel that was big enough to step into. It had stirrups for the feet and cuffs of steel that curved over the wrists, and she was soon locked into it. The first indication she had that it was suspended on a pivot only came when Bradley spun her around, brought her mouth as low as his groin, then swung her effortlessly upright again. The shock of the sudden lurch of movement, coupled with the bleakness of her outlook, made the terrified girl burst into desolate sobs.

'What do you think of her, Bradley?' Lady Bradburn asked, looking speculatively from the shocked girl to her chauffeur.

'I think she's very nice, ma'am.' Bradley looked hungrily at the trussed girl.

'And what about these?' Lady Bradburn took hold of Poppy's white blouse and wrenched it up, some of the buttons popping off and rattling on the floor, until the girl's breasts were vulnerably exposed. With a calculated smile she then turned Poppy's nipples in her fingertips and stared deep into Bradley's eyes. 'Would you like to play with them too?' she purred.

'Yes, ma'am, of course I would, very much.' Bradley approached Poppy's nipples with a different touch, flicking them with the balls of his thumbs. His tongue appeared as he licked his lips, staring hard at Poppy. 'And I wouldn't mind giving them a good suck, too.'

The woman laughed musically. 'Go ahead, then,' she cooed, 'be my guest. Make the most of her; she'll not be with us for very much longer.'

'No, stop,' Poppy cried, trying vainly to escape even though she knew they could twist and turn and manipulate her to their will. But bravely she turned her head and looked directly into Lady Bradburn's eyes, challenging her. 'I'm not an *object* for you to use as you feel like doing!'

'But that's *exactly* what you are, Cavendish,' the woman chuckled.

As Bradley started to lick and suck Poppy's nipples, making them stiffen traitorously, Lady Bradburn lifted the girl's skirt and tugged her knickers down, exposing her sex. 'What about this, Bradley?' She pulled Poppy's sex lips apart between two fingers, a momentary gleam of pink flesh between silky, curling hairs. 'Does this little morsel turn you on too?'

Poppy began twisting her midriff from side to side, as much to escape the growing feelings of pleasure that radiated from her sexual region as to avoid Lady Bradburn's inspection of it. But alas, her desperate struggling did more to encourage Lady Bradburn and her henchman than to dissuade them.

'Yes, ma'am.' Bradley answered Lady Bradburn's question by rubbing his uniformed groin with his palm, and the two females stared in fascination at the hard lump that had arisen there. 'I wouldn't mind fucking her, ma'am, I must say.'

'No,' Poppy cried, her conscious mind vying for superiority over her pussy as it signalled its excitement at the prospect of being penetrated by Bradley's rigid organ.

'And what about this, Bradley?'

Poppy's head and stomach span as Lady Bradburn swivelled her body, leaving her hanging upside-down in the wickedly ingenious contraption. Then the cunning woman leant down a little and with her tongue protruding, lapped across the girl's exposed clitoris, savouring the flavour and fragrance like a fine wine connoisseur. 'Am I making you feel horny?' she gloated at the servant.

'I'll say, ma'am!' Bradley enthused, crudely jerking his hips forward, and there was no disguising the stiffness of the flesh that bulged in his trousers even before Lady Bradburn pulled down his zip and drew it out. Its bulbous helmet was deeply purple and glowed with such carnality that it simply took Poppy's breath away as it throbbed with intent before her upturned face. She licked her lips nervously, uncertain what would happen next as Lady Bradburn drew the foreskin back and forth, alternately revealing and covering the plum-head, and looked at Bradley expectantly.

Poppy watched with her own shameful passions ever increasing as Lady Bradburn bent, right in front of the girl's wide eyes, to swallow his cock, which stood at a proud upward angle from his opened trousers. From simply watching the erotic act, and hearing the wet sucking noises from the woman's active mouth and their mutual moans of ardour, Poppy found herself rising towards an intense climax, and perhaps it was being hopelessly bound and not able to take part that fuelled her excitement.

Lady Bradburn allowed his stiff column to bob free from her skilful lips and tongue. 'Enough of this little lame brain,' she panted huskily. 'Little bimbos like Cavendish are ten-a-penny. There'll be a couple more arriving very soon, and I might let you play with them if you're good.' She kissed him fervently. 'A mature woman with wealth and brains is far harder to find, and impossible to replace,' she added sensuously.

Then the two burst into a flurry of passionate activity. Lady Bradburn grabbed his shoulders and pulled him back to the wall behind her. 'Fuck me now,' she hissed, wrapping her arms around his neck and a leg around his waist. 'Fuck me as hard as you can!'

'Yes, ma'am,' he grunted through gritted teeth, scrabbling with her clothes and then rutting violently against her pinned body.

'Oh yes!' she urged, throwing her head back against the wall and staring wide-eyed up at the shadowy ceiling, her fingers tugging on his hair like talons. 'Yes! Yes!'

From her upturned position Poppy couldn't really make out any details, but the fervour of their passion was almost tangible. The way he aggressively buffeted the woman's body against the wall as he fucked her looked painful to the watching girl, but the woman was clearly in blissful rapture.

It was soon over, Bradley groaning into Lady Bradburn's shoulder as he came, the lady wrapping her other leg around his waist and squeezing him tight to her sandwiched body. In the shadows they stood heaving against each other, until she lowered her feet to the floor and the spent chauffeur slumped away from her.

'Thank you, Bradley,' the woman said, her haughty poise immediately restored as she straightened and adjusted her clothes, then patted her hair into perfect place, 'that was very nice.'

As the chauffeur did up his trousers, now looking clumsily out of his depth, he nodded and murmured an obsequious reply Poppy didn't catch.

Lady Bradburn then moved to the bound girl and spun her smoothly upright in the frame. 'Now,' she purred, like a cat toying with a little bird, 'I'm going to leave you alone here for a while to reflect on your situation. I would advise you to take this opportunity for some quiet reflection to come to terms with your destiny and accept it with good grace; it will make life in the future far more bearable for you. And there's no point making any noise while you're here; the room is soundproofed.' She laughed gaily, gave Poppy a very light kiss on the lips, and then turned with her head and shoulders held high and waved condescendingly for Bradley to follow her from the grim room, locking the door as they left Poppy in shadowy, frightening solitude.

Poppy lost all track of time, slumped in the frame, her legs and arms aching, her fringe stuck damply to her perspiring forehead. She drifted in and out of consciousness, losing touch with the reality of where she was, sometimes thinking she was back at Maidenhall, giggling and enjoying herself with Karen, and sometimes imagining she was in a rundown old riverside cottage, or in an alley masturbating Robert Bradburn...

Eventually the door opened, and Poppy, feeling numb, wearily lifted her eyes to see who it was.

Lady Bradburn had returned, accompanied by Captain Smythe and a swarthy, portly man. Poppy guessed immediately that this was the dreaded Hamid. Time really had run out for her.

'Well, Cavendish,' the captain said, slapping his leather driving gloves against his thigh, 'it's nearing that time.'

Many a girl would have given in to hopelessness then and crumbled, but Poppy strove to look beyond her current predicament, perilous though it clearly was, and just prey that some chink of hope would emerge, steeling herself to be ready to grasp any opportunity to escape, no matter how fleeting that opportunity might be.

'I've some wonderful news for you, Cavendish,' Lady Bradburn said. 'This is Mr Hamid. You've heard us talking about him, I'm sure.' She gave Poppy a probing look, seeming to closely monitor her reactions to what she was hearing.

'I-I don't think so, ma'am,' Poppy replied, furrowing her brow in apparent mystification.

'Well, that doesn't matter.' Captain Smythe and Mr Hamid exchanged a meaningful glance as Lady Bradburn went on, 'You're very lucky. Mr Hamid has a young nephew. He's very rich and he's looking for a wife. We've sent him your photograph and he wants you to be his bride.' She paused expectantly.

'This is too good an opportunity for you to miss,' Captain Smythe said. 'We'd be failing in our duty if we didn't send you.'

'Why is she already restrained?' Mr Hamid butted in. 'Has she been giving you trouble?'

'Not at all,' the captain said smoothly, 'she merely wished to demonstrate her level of submission to us.' He put his face close to Poppy's so that the visitor could not see it, and frowned so sternly that she trembled. 'Isn't that right, Miss Cavendish?'

'Yes, sir.' Guessing that her survival might depend on how she handled the next few minutes, Poppy looked at Mr Hamid with frightened eyes. 'I try to be a good girl at all times, sir, and always do exactly as I'm told.'

'You say that,' Hamid commented sternly, 'but how can I be sure?'

'How about a firsthand demonstration?' Lady Bradburn suggested, adding generously, 'You can give her a thorough caning, if you like. Then you'll see how well she responds to some healthy discipline.'

Hamid pondered the offer for a few moments, Poppy watching him fearfully, breathlessly awaiting his response.

'Very well,' he eventually decided. 'Have her taken to the apartment. In accordance with our usual instructions, she has her college uniform with her?'

The conniving couple nodded enthusiastically. 'Yes, Hamid, of course she does.

'Very good,' he said, and then turned his nose up a little as he looked her sweating body up and down. 'Have her showered and waiting for me in her uniform.'

'I'll get one of the staff to see to it straightaway,' Lady Bradburn fawned.

'Good.' Hamid nodded curtly, not a flicker of compassion in his dark eyes. 'And in the meantime I would like to enjoy a glass of sherry in the sitting room.'

'Of course!' the couple blurted together, almost tripping over each other in their eagerness to following closely behind as he turned and left the room without another look at the bound girl.

Poppy watched the door closing, and heard Captain Smythe ask, 'What time's your sailing, Hamid?'

'Friday evening, from Tilbury,' the man replied, 'assuming the financial side completes in time.'

'We'll check our numbered account by telephone,' Lady Bradburn said, and then the door sealed and Poppy heard no more...

Half an hour later she stood nervously beside one of the armchairs in the apartment. It was early evening, and although she desperately wanted to make her getaway, she knew Hamid could well appear at any moment and catch her with the duplicate key unlocking the French windows, and that really would blow forever any meagre chance she had of getting away.

And she was right, because no sooner had she glanced wistfully at the French windows, than the door unlocked and Hamid appeared, gripping a thick cane that made Poppy's stomach churn, and closely followed by the two sycophants, Captain Smythe and Lady Bradburn.

'As you can see, Miss Cavendish,' Hamid said pompously, 'I am a traditionalist.' He tested the cane again, with the practiced air of an artisan. 'I like the cane for its simplicity, as well as for the ascetic purity of the stripes it makes on unpunished flesh.'

Captain Smythe and Lady Bradburn swapped anxious glances, for they knew her flesh most definitely was not unpunished, but they both murmured their agreement of his penchants.

He moved closer to Poppy, and used the tip of the cane to tap each of her breasts in turn. Then moving his face intimidatingly close to hers, he asked, 'What do you deserve most in the world at this moment?'

'I... I deserve to be punished, sir.' She bent dutifully without waiting to be told, and her glossy hair swept down to the carpet. Her round buttocks were pristine and peach-like in the snug comfort of the white panties she wore, and as she offered them for punishment she felt the back of her skirt being lifted.

'Nice underwear, I see.' Hamid's tone was clearly one of great approval, his hand moved between her slightly parted legs and his fingertips gently stroked and squeezed her hidden sex lips, the delicate shape of which could just be defined through the sheer white material.

'I see that you are already a little wet,' he observed, his voice deep and surprisingly gentle. Soft liquid noises, barely audible in the breathless atmosphere of the room, confirmed the condition of Poppy's duplicitous body.

'In my country it is not decorous for a woman to lubricate prematurely,' he stated, 'and so for this shameful reaction it is only right that you must be punished.' His middle finger slid against the valley of her sex and located the little hidden bud of pleasure there, making her wince with bliss.

'I do hope this cunt has not been penetrated?' he said, his tone suddenly more aggressive. Nobody dared commit to an answer.

'You may leave us alone for a while,' he said, looking up at Captain Smythe and Lady Bradburn, and they dutifully left the apartment.

The cane was administered coldly and with terrific force, on her buttocks and across the tops of her creamy thighs. As the pain of the onslaught made her sob plaintively, she felt the tips of Hamid's fingers tracing a circular path around her clitoral area. 'I suppose this is the kind of activity you engage in when alone, is it?'

'Yes sir,' Poppy gasped, unable to prevent her thighs from shaking as pleasure streamed through her. 'I-I'm sorry, sir. I know it's naughty of me...'

Although his tone had made it clear that he considered the touching of her pussy shameful, Hamid's caress did not cease, but instead grew more intense. The pain of her punishment had made Poppy's earlier excitement ebb away, but as his hand moved between her legs her pleasure quickly returned. Then her punishment was both immediate and stringent.

'Oh, sir!' the girl pleaded, tears dripping from her eyes to the carpet at her feet as pain striped her lower buttocks and upper thighs. 'No more, I beg you!'

'What about *these?*' Hamid stepped around to her front, and she noticed the stubby promontory of erect flesh that protruded in the front of his trousers as he opened her shirt and freed her breasts, neatly encased in her lacy bra. 'I suppose you are not above playing with your nipples too, like this?'

As his fingers seized the tips of her breasts and pinched them, the front of his trousers touched her face and she felt the hardness of the penis beneath the material.

'Yes, Mr Hamid, I do,' she confessed. 'But please forgive me for being so lewd, sir.'

'Forgive you? I think not.' Hamid's tone was one of moral indignation. 'If I do that you may go on to greater acts of licentiousness. What you need, my girl, is some thorough discipline.'

Poppy wailed as her bottom reddened under the fusillade of blows, a barrage that did not cease until Hamid was breathing heavily from the exertion, and then he lowered the cane and hastily tugged opened his trousers with his free hand. 'Open you mouth,' he said harshly, and as soon as Poppy's lips hesitantly parted he shoved his plump cock into her wet warm mouth without ceremony. Then he started to move his hips methodically, his expression blank, no hint of emotion there, and within a minute or two he ejaculated deep into the bent girl's throat, holding the back of her head tight and pressing his corpulent belly against her hot face until she had swallowed every last drop of his viscous seed.

Then he released her and walked to the door as she slowly straightened up, watching his back as she wiped her lips with the back of her hand. He opened the door and then turned. 'Get a good night's sleep,' he told her. 'You'll need as much rest as you can get.'

Although desperate to make her escape, and barely daring or able to believe a chink of an opportunity had in fact presented itself, Poppy risked waiting until the house seemed particularly still and quiet. It was dark outside by now, so too anxious to even think about changing into her jeans and T-shirt in case someone came back and found her wearing them while she timed her getaway, she took the key and money from their hiding place, breathing a huge sigh of relief that they were still nestled there, and dashed quietly for the French window.

Sixty seconds later she was squeezing through the gap in the hedge, and then dashing as fast as her legs would carry her along the pavement towards Burchester. She hoped buses were still running to Maidenhall at such a late hour, although she was wary of using public transport for fear of being spotted by someone.

She could perhaps try to find a taxi office, but this option also concerned her because she couldn't be sure just how interwoven the Bradburn tendrils were into the fabric of Burchester.

It would probably be safer to use her thumb.

As Poppy climbed out of the car in Maidenhall's small high street, she failed to notice the way the driver's eyes, illuminated by the orange light from the dashboard, followed the subtle movement of her breasts, and then her bottom and her shapely legs with regretful longing.

As she turned and bent to look through the open passenger car door window to thank him for the lift, she did notice how his brooding eyes latched on to the gap in her shirt and devoured her deep cleavage, and this realisation unsettled her.

'Are you sure you won't get back in?' the man asked ominously.

'No, thank you,' Poppy told him, 'this is as far as I want to go.'

'Aww, come on,' he said as she turned and started to walk quickly away from the car, only to be aware that it started prowling slowly behind her. 'How about thanking me properly?' he called out of the lowered window. 'Don't you think it's rude not to show me your appreciation?'

'No,' Poppy said, turning to look over her shoulder, 'now go away and leave me alone *oh?!*'

Poppy was aware of the car's engine revving and the vehicle accelerating away from the kerb and into the night along the high street as she rebounded off the muscular chest she'd just clattered into. Her immediate instinct was that she'd again bumped into Robert Bradburn. 'Let me go!' she shrieked, tears of frustration and fear springing instantly to her eyes. '*Please!* I can't take any more!'

'It's all right,' a strong voice said, 'it's all right.' And when she looked up she saw, through sparkling teardrops, a pleasant face framed by dark curly hair. She blinked to clear her vision and recognised Jeff Riley, the young man who had run after Captain Smythe's car just a few days before. 'Nobody's going to hurt you, Penelope,' he said with a comforting smile. 'Nobody's going to hurt you ever again.'

Chapter 10

'Has he gone?' Poppy asked, pressing her body close to Jeff Riley's as she cowered behind his muscular form. As agitated as she was, the fact that he'd used a name as though he knew her completely eluded the girl. Her hands trembled as they clutched at his shirt, and her expression was one of desperate anxiety.

'Yes, he's gone,' he said reassuringly.

'H-have they followed me?'

'Who?' Jeff stared at her with an expression of bemusement.

'Captain Smythe and Lady Bradburn!' she said, as though he was stupid for asking such a daft question.

'*Captain* Smythe? *Lady* Bradburn?' Jeff shook his head in disbelief, and Poppy could not help noticing how handsome he was. 'I don't know what they've been telling you, but it sounds as if that pair are suffering from delusions of grandeur. You'd better come and have a little chat with my mother, Penelope.'

'Why do you call me that?' she asked, but he did not reply. Instead he took her hand in his and led her into *The Bowman's Arms*.

After Captain Smythe's previously dire warnings about the place Poppy felt some trepidation, but the warmth of the interior was welcoming and the atmosphere cosy as Jeff took her through to a low-beamed bar filled with a few drinkers. There was a brief cessation to the murmurs of conversation while the drinkers eyed the gorgeous newcomer in a school uniform, as Jeff led her over to a matronly woman sitting behind the bar casting an all-seeing eye over her domain.

'Look who I found wandering outside, mum,' he said, and Mrs Riley got up from her stool as her son went on. 'From what I can gather so far she's got away from Smythe and Bradburn somehow, and she needs our help.'

Jeff's mother put a sturdily protective arm around Poppy's shoulder and looked into her eyes with genuine compassion, as she signalled to her son that it was time to start dispersing the last of the patrons. 'Let's get you upstairs, my dear,' said the comely woman.

'Come on, you lot,' Jeff called, turning to the stragglers still drinking. 'You've had your little lock-in. It's late and time you were getting home to your beds.'

'But I must get to Maidenhall,' Poppy insisted to the landlady. 'My friends might be in danger!'

Upstairs, Mrs Riley bustled about finding a dressing gown and preparing a quick meal to fortify the girl, the smell of which made Poppy realise just how famished she really was. Then as Poppy sat at the kitchen table eating with gusto and sipping appreciatively from the mug of steaming hot tea set down beside her, the woman brought out a photo album.

'Have a look at these, my dear,' she said.

'Poppy,' the girl said, swallowing a tasty mouthful of beans on toast. 'My name's Poppy... Poppy Cavendish. Why did Jeff call me Penelope?'

'Because your name's not Poppy Cavendish, it's Penelope Bowman.' Mrs Riley dropped the bombshell, carefully watching for the girl's reaction, and a forkful of beans hovered in front of Poppy's open mouth.

What on earth were the pair talking about? What was all this nonsense? They clearly had her mistaken for someone else.

Jeff peeled a photo out of the album and put it before her on the tabletop. 'Take a look at this,' he said.

'But...' Poppy felt weird as she stared at a woman who could have been a slightly older version of her, except that the clothes were slightly dated and she was standing beside a baby in a pram. 'Who... who is she?' she asked, although a gut feeling told her she already knew the attractive female. 'I don't understand.'

'*That's* you.' Mrs Riley pointed at the baby's wispy auburn hair. 'Penelope, your parents named you. That's your mother.' She moved her pointing finger to the woman. 'And this is your father, Captain Charles Bowman.' She slid a photograph of a dashing young army officer across the table. 'They were both killed in a tragic car smash not long after this picture was taken.' Mrs Riley paused, hoping the enormity of what she was saying would sink in without too much distress. 'You're a rich young lady, Penelope, heiress to the Bowman estate.'

Poppy sat in silence for a long time, staring blankly at the two pictures. It was all too much for the girl to take in, but with great restraint she managed to calmly place the knife and fork on the plate, even as tears that squeezed from the corners of her eyes betrayed the effect the enormity of what she was hearing and seeing was having on her.

Jeff went down and fetched her a brandy from the bar, and after a hot bath his mother put the exhausted and emotionally numbed girl to bed in the spare room.

A short while later Poppy awoke, unexpectedly feeling troubled, and padding out of the unfamiliar bedroom she found mother and son in the lounge of the living accommodation above the pub.

Mrs Riley gently explained that after the tragic death of Poppy's parents Bowman Hall had been taken over by a private company and converted into Maidenhall College. Prior to that Mrs Riley had worked up at Bowman Hall, and showed Poppy photographs of a couple who were sadly killed with them, her father's friend, Captain Desai and his attractive English wife.

'My friend Suky Desai is being kept prisoner up at the college, I'm sure of it!' Poppy exploded, suddenly shaking herself out of the numbing torpor she had felt since hearing the sorry news. 'She must be their daughter!'

Mrs Riley nodded, while Jeff showed Poppy a staff photograph taken at Bowman Hall shortly before the crash.

'I-I can't believe I'm seeing this.' Poppy's vision swam with tears as she took in the familiar faces and the inscriptions written beneath them. '*Charles's batman, Corporal Smythe,*' she read aloud, '*with their chauffeur and parlour maid, the Bradburns.* Does this mean what I think it means?' she asked.

Mrs Riley nodded. 'You've been usurped, my dear. We've had our suspicions about what's been going on at the old hall ever since the takeover, with who was previously the batman suddenly elevated to a position of authority. Something smacked of corruption, but with no proof what could we do? We've been carefully watching and monitoring your progress from afar, and when Jeff saw you being driven off the other day the alarm bells really started to ring. But still, we could hardly go to the police with some daft conspiracy theory, could we? So we just had to hope that you were going to be okay and that our fears were as silly as they sounded.'

'But don't worry, Poppy.' Jeff squeezed her hand and gave her a reassuring smile, using the name she was familiar and comfortable with. 'You're safe now, and we'll help you get your friends out of there. And then we'll do what we can to get back what's rightfully yours, too.'

Next morning Poppy awoke to find a note from Mrs Riley on the unit bedside her bed. *Gone to get you some new clothes. Jeff will look after you.*

Still hugely bewildered by the revelations of the previous night, in going to the bathroom Poppy mistakenly pushed the wrong door open, just a little before she caught sight of a duvet thrown back and Jeff's naked upper half before her, lying on his bed, his erect penis standing up. She knew he had not seen her as she watched his fist continue to slide up and down a cock that looked harder than polished oak. As she wondered what mental image could excite him so, he panted a name aloud.

'*Penelope...*'

The girl had intended to steal away silently to the bathroom, but she found herself transfixed by the breathlessly erotic vision and by the fact that he was obviously fantasising about her.

Excitement gripped her, and despite wanting to quickly formulate and action some sort of plan to get Karen and Suky out of Maidenhall - if they were indeed being held there against their will - she could not resist giving in to temptation, and slipped a hand inside the borrowed dressing gown to her pussy, which was already damp.

But in moving her arm she accidentally nudged her elbow against the door behind which she was hiding, and she froze and watched in horror as it slowly, inexorably swung open. The movement drew Jeff's vision, and when he saw her standing there he twisted his body away in a violent paroxysm of shame.

'Jeff, please...' She took a couple of paces into the room and tried to catch his eye, but only succeeded in noticing that the embarrassment of being discovered masturbating had made his penis wilt a little. 'Jeff, I wasn't spying on, honest. I was looking for the bathroom and found your room by mistake.'

'Go away, Poppy.' Facing grimly away from her he dismissively waved his hand back in her direction. 'I'll never be able to face you again. I feel so ashamed. Please, go away and leave me alone.'

'Don't be ashamed, Jeff.' Instead of retreating from his bedroom she did the complete opposite and moved closer to his single bed, and reached down to touch his dark curly hair. 'Please.' As he looked cautiously over his shoulder her dressing gown fell open and he saw her hand, covering her pussy. 'You see, Jeff, I'm no better.' She smiled shyly. 'Can't we just enjoy ourselves together?'

'Well... would... would you like to get in with me?' he asked hopefully.

'Oh yes, I would,' she said honestly, feeling a strong need to be close to someone.

They lay face to face beneath the duvet, and when Jeff's fingers stole inside her dressing gown Poppy reached down and wrapped her fingers around his cock. Then she slipped beneath the bedclothes and took his erection in her mouth with quiet subservience. When a little salty fluid began seeping into her mouth she knew his ejaculation was near, and his fingers in her hair slowed her lips' up and down motion.

'I'll come too soon if you carry on like that, Poppy,' he panted.

'I want you inside me,' she said, and eased him on top of her, between her legs, which she raised and wrapped around his hips.

Their slow lovemaking was of considerable duration, Poppy's hands drifting over his back as his cock took her higher and higher, his hands squeezing between her and the mattress to cup her buttocks.

Eventually they climaxed together, and then lay in one another's arms, kissing and talking affectionately to each other. This was what Poppy had been looking for, and it seemed ungracious to admit to herself that there was perhaps something missing, so she suppressed the feeling as she found the bathroom at last, showered, and dressed, Mrs Riley having laid the new jeans and T-shirt she'd kindly bought for her on the bed in the spare room.

Then she sat down to breakfast with Jeff and told him of her concerns that Hamid, who would by now be fully aware of her disappearance, would take Suky and Karen in her place.

'Friday night from Tilbury, you say?' Jeff said, confirming the transportation details Poppy had vaguely overheard back at the Bradburns' house. She nodded. 'Today is Wednesday,' he went on, thinking aloud, 'so we'll have to make our move soon.'

'*Our* move?' she gasped. 'Shouldn't we just go to the police? Wouldn't that be the sensible thing to do?'

'I'm not so sure it would be, no,' he said, shaking his head. 'The Bradburns are both magistrates, and they have friends in high places - including the local police force.'

With an icy foreboding gripping her stomach, Poppy remembered Robert Bradburn's boasting about that very same thing.

'If we can call in an outside crime squad, then okay,' Jeff went on. 'But we'll have to get hold of some pretty conclusive evidence first, otherwise we'll be putting you, and perhaps Karen and Suky, in more danger than you're already in.'

He took her hand in a comfortingly strong grip. 'Tell me everything that's happened to you,' he gently encouraged. 'Don't leave anything out, no matter how insignificant it may seem now. I need to know it all.'

Poppy glanced at the kitchen door. 'Where's you mother?' she asked, not wanting to share the finer details of the whole sorry tale with too many listeners.

'Don't worry,' Jeff reassured her. 'She's busy down in the bar getting it ready with the cleaner and the pot-man. We'll be opening up soon.'

Stumbling at first, trying to piece together everything she'd been through, so much having happened in such a short space of time that she struggled at first to get them into an order of events, she told him the whole sorry story, from that first morning in her dormitory at the college when Miss Brady caught her masturbating, to her punishment by Captain Smythe and Miss Sharpe and her torrid little affair with the headmistress. Through her introduction to the Bradburns and the training by them she went, via her cruel seduction by their snake-of-a-son Robert, to eventually finding a bit of an ally in Lucy Jessop, to the duplicitous Tony luring her into the mini orgy in the tumbledown riverside cottage and then possibly enticing her into Robert Bradburn's clutches again. She missed out nothing, until she concluded with the previous day's caning by the loathsome villain who was Hamid.

'And that's about it, Jeff.' She tried to smile but only succeeded in staring at him blankly. 'Now you know everything about what I've been through. Every sordid detail.'

'Okay,' Jeff said, having spent a good half hour gazing out of the kitchen window, down at the rusty old swing and beer tables in the garden. 'I've got a plan.'

91

'You have?' Poppy said, getting more and more anxious about her two friends as every minute ticked by.

'Yep,' he said determinedly, turning to look at her sitting at the table. 'We'll go up there, to Maidenhall, you and me, and if we do find Karen and Suky in the infirmary we'll set them free, and then do some snooping around to see what we can find out about what's been going on there.'

Poppy waited silently for a moment, looking at him expectantly, waiting for the real *coup de grâce* of his brilliant and intricately thought out strategy. 'And...?' she gently encouraged.

'And?' he said, looking a little deflated at her muted reaction.

'And, what happens then?'

'Well... as I said, we find out what we can.'

'Yes, and then what?'

'Um, well then we expose them.'

'And that's it?'

'Yep.'

'But it's broad daylight! Someone's bound to see us.'

'We'll be okay. As you know there's only a skeleton staff on during the summer holidays. And the vast majority of the girls are away. Besides, if we wait till dark it might put your friends in more danger than they're possibly already in.'

Poppy couldn't deny the truth of that remark. 'Yes, I understand that, but—'

'Have you got a better idea?'

Poppy pondered their other options for a moment, very quickly concluded that they didn't actually have any, and then said, 'No, when do we go?'

Walking across the sunny fields at the back of the pub, following a shortcut known to Jeff, Poppy was surprised to discover that the college was only half a mile away as the crow flies. The morning was warm and peaceful and Poppy wished she didn't have such a weight of responsibility on her shoulders, such a potentially dangerous mission to accomplish, which was spoiling any chance of her enjoying the beauty of the day, the countryside, and the man she was with.

She knew a section of Maidenhall College's tall perimeter wall where there was a locked metal gate and an overhanging bough, and using these two aids in conjunction made the climb a lot easier than it might have been. Jeff scrabbled up first, and then leant back to help Poppy up, then they both jumped down and scurried immediately into a thicket, out of sight of the main buildings.

It all went unbelievably smoothly, and this only sharpened their despair when two people stepped in their path as they made their way across the stretch of open lawn between the wall and the main body of the college. Poppy's heart sank as she saw the stern countenances of Miss Sharpe and Neville Bradburn, the latter holding a shotgun, which he pointed in their direction.

'You'll have to kill the both of us if you want to stop us getting inside.' Jeff, who had grown up poaching with his dad and knew all about firearms, stood bravely in front of the girl, but Poppy stepped to his side, set on showing the pair that she was as determined as he was to complete what they'd come for. 'There's no way other way you'll stop me.'

'Stop us,' Poppy insisted, doggedly wanting to show that she was no shrinking violet either. 'There's no way you'll stop us.'

'It's not what you think!' Miss Sharpe stepped forward with her arms outstretched in surrender. 'Poppy, we're here to help you.'

'Oh, yes?' Poppy defiantly tossed back her cascade of auburn hair. 'Here to help sell me into slavery, perhaps!'

'No, please believe us, my dear.' Sir Neville turned the gun around and offered her the stock. 'We've finished with all that. Really, we have.'

'Well I won't trust you until you prove yourselves.' Jeff took the shotgun and broke it open. When he saw the brass ends of two cartridges gleaming in the breech he closed it again with practiced precision. 'We want hard evidence of what's been going on here since the death of Miss Bowman's parents.' He levelled the weapon at its former owner. 'So take us to it.'

Neville Bradburn exchanged a glance with Miss Sharpe, and with a shrug of resignation, she nodded.

'The office,' the headmistress said tightly, 'you'll find what you're looking for in there. The financial records are kept in the safe, though. I've never been allowed access to them.' She swallowed, and they could see that she was making these revelations only with an enormous effort. 'The captain keeps the keys on his person at all times. He's in the staff room with Lady Bradburn. Obviously they know Poppy's on the loose and that's why they've come back here. To regroup and decide what they're going to do about it. They detailed us off to keep a watch for her.'

'The *corporal*, you mean.' Jeff jabbed the weapon towards the college. 'Now, move!'

The administration block was on the first floor in West House, and they had to creep past the staff room to mount the stairs. They heard the murmur of voices inside as they did so, but reached the main office without incident. When Miss Sharpe produced her keys Jeff took them from her, shepherded everyone inside, closed and locked the door and pointed to a chair.

'You sit there,' he ordered Neville Bradburn, 'and keep away from the window.' Then switching on the computers that stood on one desk, he said to Miss Sharpe, 'Give Poppy the papers in chronological order, starting with those relating to her.'

Poppy hardly had a chance to glance at the information as Jeff ran them through a scanner and sent them out by e-mail, to where she did not know, but she glimpsed a birth certificate, army discharge papers and death certificates.

Later paperwork hailed from India, and when she noticed the name Desai she remembered Suky as she had last seen her before she left the college a few days earlier. Suky's father had been her own father's loyal friend, and she realised that this made a special bond between them as the names and details of Anne Maddox and Erica Pringle - two other ex-Maidenhall girls - passed through her hands, into the scanner and then out into cyberspace. Soon they delved further into the past, and saw the names of girls that had been through the college spanning many years.

'Almost finished,' Miss Sharpe said, and the hushed words were hardly out when they all froze as they heard footsteps outside and the door handle turned, fruitlessly.

'Are you in there, mother?' an arrogant voice enquired.

Poppy's blood ran cold. *It was Robert Bradburn!* As she dithered in fear and uncertainty Jeff lifted the shotgun propped against the chair he was sitting on, and signalled to Miss Sharpe to open the door. He stood behind it as she turned the key and pulled it open, and when Robert swaggered in Jeff slammed and locked it before the creep knew what was happening.

'What the fuck's going on in here?' Robert looked around in disbelief. 'Is this a burglary or something?' Then he saw Poppy and lunged towards her aggressively, snarling, 'You little bitch!' But his attempted attack proved Poppy's previous instinct about Jeff's pugilistic talents accurate, when he stepped in front of Robert and landed a sharp uppercut to his jaw. Robert's eyes rolled and glazed, he swayed for a moment like a tree about to fall, looked at Poppy with an expression of frozen shock on his face, then collapsed in a heap, sending a chair scuttling across the floor, and no sooner was he pole-axed than Poppy snapped into action and grabbed some sticky tape from the desktop and hastily secured his hands and feet, and then slapped a strip across his mouth. Jeff went through his pockets, and took out a bulging wallet and the keys to his sports car.

Giving his knuckles a rueful rub, Jeff then returned to his task and handed Poppy the last of the documents, which she placed in a folder.

Jeff nodded towards Bradburn and Sharpe. 'We'll sort them out shortly,' he said to Poppy, ushering them out of the office with a fierce glare and a jerk of the shotgun in the direction of the door, 'but first we must secure the place.' Outside on the landing he spoke to their prisoners quietly.

'You've started to prove your repentance, but you've wronged Poppy and tried to rob her of her birthright, not to mention what you've done to all those other girls.' He nodded at Neville Bradburn. 'I'm putting the pair of you in with your wife and Smythe until we decide what to do with you.'

Making their way down the stairs, Jeff stealthily leading the little convoy, Poppy taking up the rear, Jeff kicked the staff room door open and marched Neville and Sharpe inside. Smythe and Caroline Bradburn looked up, a frozen tableau of disbelief.

'Right, listen to me, you shower of shit.' Jeff pointed to the bulky folder under Poppy's arm. 'I've spent the last half an hour e-mailing the details of your crimes to my computer at home. Those details will have already been backed-up by my mother and put into safekeeping, so, in effect, we've got you all by the bollocks and you're in big trouble, believe me.

'Now,' he went on, 'I want you to be very, very quiet for as long as it takes me to peruse your financial activities over the last seventeen years. If you co-operate, who knows? You may not end up in jail. On the other hand if you don't co-operate, well, I think you understand me.'

'How *dare* you?' Having got over his initial shock, the man Poppy still thought of as *Captain* Smythe rose up in fury. 'What the devil?!' he stormed, his expression one of apoplexy. 'You'd better hand over that gun right now, you little runt, before?'

There was a deafening bang, and the acrid odour of a fired shotgun cartridge quickly filled the room. The lead shot splattered the ceiling and plaster rained down on the dumbfounded figures of Smythe and his accomplices, covering their heads and shoulders like icing sugar.

'You're a serial kidnapper, Smythe,' Jeff said calmly. 'One step nearer to Miss Bowman and I'll blast your guts all over the wall behind you. And don't thing I wouldn't. When I get angry I tend to act first and consider the consequences later. And I'm angry right now. So hand over the keys to the safe.'

Smythe looked a shadow of his former self and could be seen to be physically intimidated by the forthright threat of the younger man, as he fell back into his chair and gasped weakly, 'Y-you're going to take my keys?'

'No.' Jeff held out his hand. 'I'm going to take Miss Bowman's keys, to see what secrets you've been hiding in her safe for all these years.'

'And while we're doing that,' Poppy said, speaking up with renewed confidence, thoroughly impressed by Jeff's complete control of the quartet and the situation, 'there are some things you might like to discuss.' She turned to the Bradburns. 'Did you know, for example, that Smythe and Old Sharpie took full advantage of *all* the girls in their care before they reached you?'

As a murmur of reproach grumbled she turned to Smythe. 'And did *you* know that Sharpie had a good time with them on her own too, behind your back?'

As Smythe glared accusingly at the now ex-headmistress, Poppy went on. 'And were any of you aware that Robert was routinely deflowering us if he got the chance to once we got to Burchester, which is why Hamid was complaining so much?' The murmur of disbelief grew louder.

'Oh, he's not *your* son, by the way,' Poppy said to Neville Bradburn, smiling at him sweetly. 'No, he's Smythe's.'

Catching her a little by surprise, Neville Bradburn actually smiled ruefully back at her. 'Thank you, my dear,' he said. 'You've done me a great favour; I've always loathed the good-for-nothing leech. And to think I've always criticised myself for thinking I'd sired such an arrogant little shit!'

'It's all lies!' Caroline Bradburn wailed desperately. 'No, it's all lies!'

'And lies are something *you* know all about,' Poppy said with a chuckle, enjoying dropping yet another little bomb. 'After all, you've also been screwing your chauffeur behind Smythe's back for ages.'

With this parting shot Poppy, feeling extremely satisfied, followed Jeff out, and he locked the door. They paused for a moment to listen to the hubbub of accusation and counter accusation going on in the room, then returned to the office and opened the safe, from which they unearthed a mine of incriminating information. Poppy was utterly appalled by the paucity of her usurpers. The college and the house in Burchester alone were worth quite a few million, and they had missed no opportunity to make as much dishonest cash out of them as they could.

'The infirmary!' she suddenly shrieked, looking aghast. 'I'd forgotten about Karen and Suky! Come on, Jeff, we must see if they're locked up in there!'

The two lovely girls were indeed locked in the old infirmary, lying in their underwear on the bed when Poppy and Jeff burst in. They drew apart hastily, and Karen's eyes widened incredulously when she saw who the intruders were. 'Poppy?' she gasped.

The three girls ran into each other's arms and hugged tightly, laughing and crying and kissing, while Jeff took a backseat for a few minutes and watched from the fringes, letting them share their moment of happy reunion.

When their joy had been expressed for the moment, he spoke to Poppy. 'You make sure your friends are okay,' he said. 'I'm going to Burchester to see if Hamid is still there or if he's crawled back under the stone he came from. And if he's still there, I'll see what he has to say for himself...'

www.ingramcontent.com/pod-product-compliance
Lightning Source LLC
Chambersburg PA
CBHW030501130626
46549CB00007B/2819